Egypt Eyes. Copyright © Roy Lester Pond 2012

ABOUT THE BLOG OF ANSON HUNTER, Alternative Egyptologist

My blog is like an archaeological dig site. The material of today lies on the surface and what lies hidden beneath is the past. Editing has allowed me to reverse the dramatic order of this story and add the benefits of evaluated experience. It has also allowed me to begin this account with a prologue – the turning point discovery that I have been led by a young blind woman into a conspiracy about the ancient past that could affect all of humankind.

1

Prologue: Walking into trouble

Sanctuary, Temple of Philae

What happened in the Temple of Isis today?

I stepped straight out of the dimly lit sanctuary and into a meaty hand that clamped around my mouth. The hand muffled my gasp as I was yanked aside.

I am rangy, yet I was dragged along like a piece of furniture, the hot salty palm preventing me from making a sound. My surprise removal ended in a darker side chamber.

As a controversial alternative Egyptologist, who also occasionally takes small tour groups around Egypt, I am always walking into trouble, but this was physical.

I had been the last out of the sanctuary, the footsteps of my small group fading in the distance, when I walked into my abduction.

"You're okay," the human gag said, taking his hand away. "Don't make a noise. We need to talk, privately."

It was a swarthy, good-looking young man I had seen walking around outside the temple. He'd got here pretty fast, then I saw another arrive and now there were two of them blocking my way out of the chamber. In fact two of *him*. Twins.

"That's a good trick being in two places at once," I said.

"We find it useful," the new arrival said.

Identical twins? No, not quite. The second one was a faintly milder version. It's a curious thing about twins, even so-called identical ones. One of them always looks more defined than the other, as if the printer cartridge is running low on ink for the second iteration.

"What, collectively, do you want from me?"

"Your help," they said together.

"I'm afraid you're going to have to hijack another guide. I've already been hired to show someone else around."

A flicker of a smile touched the face of the milder-looking of the two.

"Yes, we know you're an alternative Egyptologist who has been hired by Dr Constance Somers, a satellite archaeologist who is now blind. But what do you know..."

"...about her? Tell us why she would hire you," the dark-print twin said, not so much ending his brother's sentence as shutting it down.

"What do you know about me that you think I'd want to tell you?"

"We know quite a bit more about you than you think..."

"You've consulted with US Intelligence in the past," hard-edged twin said.

This is no secret. I've blogged about it.

"Who are you?"

Twin Lite said softly: "Let's say US surveillance."

"What sort of surveillance?"

"That doesn't matter. The fact is, Dr Somers may have stumbled on something that could have far reaching repercussions and implications..."

Dr Constance Somers is celebrated for her work in satellite archaeology before she went blind. Am I now her eye on the ground, where once she had a satellite eye in the sky?

Who are these two on her trail?

Having worked with Intelligence organizations in the past, I have heard of the National Reconnaissance Office or NRO. It was once a classified agency of the US Department of Defence and its existence was flatly denied until recent times. NRO designs, builds and works with the Air Force, operating the US reconnaissance intelligence satellites. Nothing on the planet is beyond the NRO's prying eyes in the sky, or beyond. Conspiracy theorists on the Internet accuse the organisation of covering-up their monitoring of unidentified objects.

"So she stumbled across something she shouldn't?" I said.

"We can't specify the nature of our investigation. But we're asking you to keep us in the picture if you learn anything or anyone approaches her. The very fact that she hired you to accompany her would suggest to us that she is acting unusually..."

"...and we know of your past history of unorthodox investigation," the other one finished his sentence.

"Why don't you talk to her?"

"She's uncooperative."

"She's keeping a secret?"

"We believe so."

"If it's such a secret how did you get onto it?"

"That's not really important right now…"

"…what matters now is that you say nothing to anyone and just keep your ears open. Others may try to reach her. Dr Somers has attracted the interest of groups that want to discover what she knows."

So they want me to be their ears and she wants me to be her eyes.

I had the feeling that the walls of the chamber were closing in.

"Why should I help you? She's asked me to be a guide and so I think my loyalty should be to her."

"Maybe it will change your mind if we tell you something. One of our investigators was tracking her and then disappeared. Dr Somers found something hidden beneath Saqqara, and he followed her down there, but only she came out. She is playing on your well-known interest in dangers from the ancient past. We think she plans to take you, without warning you, into an environment with unknown but lethal hazards. We don't want you vanishing too…"

"So you'd better have this," the harder one said.

"What's that?"

"A tracking device so that we can come if you vanish too."

He handed me a small object about half the size of a flash-drive stick.

I was puzzled enough to accept it and to slip it into a pocket.

"Don't say anything to her. Just keep an ear to the ground. We'll get back to you down the track."

Egypt eyes

I'm here in Aswan, Egypt, researching one of my theories about the ancient past for a new book, when out of the blue I get an invitation to show a young blind woman around Egypt.

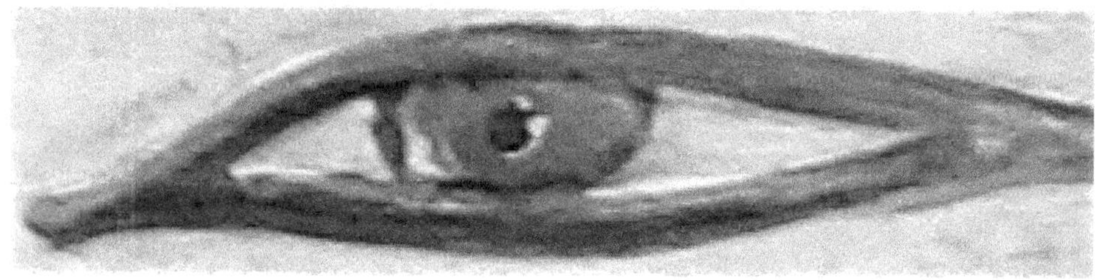

"Be my eyes in Egypt," she said.

I always like the sense of being drawn into intrigue and in this case my sensors are resonating like ground-penetrating radar. Also, I have a flexibility reflex that keeps getting me into trouble. It lures me into accepting dubious propositions and offers of employment that help to fund my investigations in Egypt.

So there I was at The Old Cataract, the hotel where Agatha Christie penned her novel Death on the Nile. I entered the gardened swimming pool area, which sits below a wide veranda with its famous cliff-top view over the rock-strewn Nile at Aswan.

I found the blind young woman relaxing on a poolside lounger.

"Hello, I'm Anson Hunter," I said, approaching her. She turned up her blonde head and her reflective dark glasses sent flashes like empty mirrors.

"Thanks for coming to meet me, Anson. I know you've taken groups around Egypt in the past and I am wondering... will you allow me to hire you as my personal guide for a week or so? I want you to be my eyes in Egypt."

"Are you sure you need me?" I said.

Old Cataract Hotel

"You're thinking a guide dog might be a better idea, perhaps Anubis, the dog god of the necropolis? No, it's you I want."

It's hard to believe now that even though I was standing right over her at the poolside, I was probably just an elongated smudge in her vision. Her female Egyptian assistant, who had emailed me, explained that Dr Constance Somers has degenerative *retinitis pigmentosa* and is now ninety percent blind. I think that's being generous.

"Me show you Egypt?" I said, squinting against the southern Egyptian sunlight. "How does that work?"

She smiled. "How do you show Egypt to a blind person?"

"I wasn't thinking that."

"Then what? You're wondering how you'd nursemaid a blind woman around Egypt? Don't worry. As you know, I have an assistant, Saneya, to look after me when I really need help. She's up there on the veranda trying to read a book, but watching me in case I get up and dive into the shallow end of the pool or something. Mostly I manage pretty well on my own with my cane, except when I'm walking in a crowded street in a city like Cairo and somebody bumps my shoulder and I'm spun around, then I don't know which way I'm facing anymore and that can be interesting."

"That's not it, either," I said, glancing at the long white cane lying on the grass beside her lounger. "At the risk of stating the obvious, you're a trained Egyptologist as well as being the world's leading space archaeologist."

"And that's your concern?"

"Yes. What could I possibly show you?"

"You're different. You don't see my condition, all you see are my qualifications."

Well, that wasn't exactly true, I thought. I saw other things about her.

I've been spending a lonely time at sites lately, poking around Aswan on the trail of one of the sons of Rameses, so I couldn't help but notice the litheness of her figure revealed by the stretchy scraps of black spandex and imagine secret areas of humidity beneath. The tremor of tightness I felt in my stomach gave way to a twinge of guilt and I felt bad for looking.

This was like stealing from an unattended store.

There's a voyeuristic aspect to staring at someone who doesn't know it and the experience is further tainted by a sense of guilt when you're looking at a person with a disability, albeit one as attractive as all hell.

I found her relaxing on a poolside lounger.

"Granted, I know Egypt," she said. "Or at least one dimension of it.

But I want you to show me something different, the unknown, unseen Egypt. Isn't that what you specialise in as an alternative Egyptologist, a phenomenologist who experiences the sacred of ancient Egypt?"

I've taken unusual people on tours of Egypt before, New Agers, neo-pagans, fundamentalists, even Intelligence community people, but the cool, slender-faced blonde, Doctor Constance Somers, is in a class of her own. Yet here she is, a celebrated Egyptologist, saying that she wants to find exactly the same thing that I do, the hidden Egypt.

But something else got in the way of her proposal besides her medical condition or her skills set. She was asking me to drop my personal research and investigations in order to accompany her.

"I'll pay you well for your time," she said. "I am not entirely a sad case. Unlike most members of my profession, I do have a dollar to scratch myself with. I inherited, you see. It took away the desire to find treasures in Egypt and I could concentrate on finding more important things."

This well-heeled Egyptologist certainly has concentrated on finding much more important things, like her discovery of a celebrated stela of the Prince Khaemwaset at Saqqara.

I have been on the trail of the very same elusive magician prince for most of my career. Khaemwaset, son of Rameses The Great, and the world's first Egyptologist, loved to investigate and restore the monuments of the ancients, admiring the perfection of everything they made. Or so he claimed in the carved stone tablets he left behind on their monuments, 'the world's biggest museum labels'. But the princely tomb raider had other motives.

Legend told that Khaemwaset went secretly in search of forbidden knowledge and power and he developed a reputation as Egypt's greatest magician.

Maybe this invitation from Constance Somers is a stroke of good fortune for me.

It's an opportunity to work covertly from inside the tent of the profession instead of outside in the wilderness.

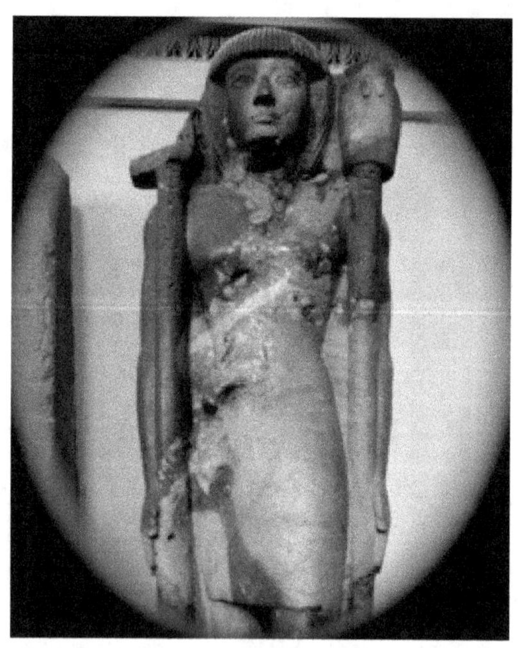

The world's first Egyptologist

My other project will have to wait. There is a secret lying buried beneath the surface of this attractive and ill-fated young academic and I am growing more and more intrigued with her.

"What do you have in mind?" I said.

"I heard you're flexible. We're going on a cruise to Luxor, to kill a little time before our new archaeological season's opening and the team's arrival. Then after that, we fly to Saqqara. We spend a week or so on site there. I'm being replaced as head of the team and this is my sort of unofficial handover. They can't have a blind academic..."

"Leading the blind academics?"

"You don't have a high opinion of us, I've heard."

"And vice versa. That's why I'm surprised you'd take the risk of associating with me. I could tarnish your reputation."

"I'll take that risk. Maybe I want you because you're a renegade."

"Intriguing."

"It may surprise you," she said, "but while I could still read, I read your blogs and your books and theories and this will be a more intimate sharing than with any other reader and no reader could feed on your words more hungrily than I will. Like The Bard's Dark Lady of the Sonnets, I'll be your lady in darkness that you can dedicate your musings to... even though I happen to be a blonde and I can still see some light and blurry shapes! Allow me to see your Egypt through your words and inspire me with the Egypt of your imagination.”

“I admit it would be a career first to have a mainstream Egyptologist hanging on my words. But I must warn you I'm no poet.”

“I'm no lady. I don't want censorship, be warned. I want your sensual reactions, too. I know you feel a powerful attraction to the feminine allure of ancient Egypt, so if something turns you on, turn me on!”

“Wow. And I felt guilty for looking at you lying there on that lounger!”

“The way you're looking at me now?”

“It does seem a bit like stealing.”

“You think I can't feel it?”

I was going to have to work at this I was beginning to learn.

“I can see this may be a bit unnerving and I could be the one walking on uncertain ground.”

“Good! That's the kind of frankness I want from you.”

Might she be hiding more than fading eyesight behind those silvery dark lenses? Maybe things were not as they seemed and this woman's request for a guided tour had a secret motive. Was a blind woman planning to lead me along some unknown path? Towards what?

"What do you look like these day, Anson?" she said. "I saw a picture of you once years ago. Describe yourself."

"Okay, I have sapphire blue eyes the colour of Brad Pitt's, or, as my ex-wife described it, I have eyes with the burning light of a fanatic. I'm about as tall as Hugh Laurie's Dr House and about as lanky as him, or in other words, a beanpole. Oh, and my hair is about the colour of George Clooney's, or going a little wintry prematurely. Does that give you a clear picture?"

"I'll judge for myself. Sit here."

I sank beside her on the edge of the lounger.

"I may have been exaggerating a bit about Brad Pitt, Hugh Laurie and George Clooney."

"Just keep your eyes closed," she said.

I obeyed.

Having your face explored by a blind person is an uncanny feeling.

You can feel your own topography emerging under those spidery fingertips, and you are conscious of your flaws.

"Try to stay on my good side."

Her fingertip examination felt like an archaeological exploration, measuring out the length of my face, surveying the mounds of my eyes and the bridge of my nose, probing the width of my mouth and the corners and the length of my chin. Perfumed, sensitive fingers. I caught the scent of an expensive sunscreen lotion, which put me in mind of ancient Egyptian unguents and priestesses in gossamer sheath dresses.

"A clever face. Amiable, flexible, yet with great constancy of purpose. Thank you, Anson."

"Will I be a great success in life?"

"I'm not telling you your fortune."

"You can go on looking."

"I've seen enough."

"There's more."

"Some people find it a little odd. But it helps if I can picture your face then I can picture your expressions."

"Okay, then now it's my turn. I'll start with a wide-ranging field survey, beginning with the toes and then working my way up to the top. Would you like me to add some sunscreen on you as I go along?"

"You're going to be fun, but no thanks. And I am not an archaeological dig site."

That was her opinion. "So tell me, are there going to be just three of us on our little tour?"

Her reply was a blow. "More. There will also be my partner, Virgil.

Virgil Powell. Virgil is… different. More like you. He's on the fringes."

My imaginings, running unhindered like an empty tomb passage, ended abruptly in an unexpected wall.

There's a partner. I hate that term. Does it mean a business partner?

No, Egyptologists don't have business partners. Of course she has a partner. She is blindingly attractive.

"Shouldn't this partner be showing you Egypt?"

She shook her head. "Virgil does not have your grasp of Egyptian sites, tombs and hidden mysteries. His expertise is elsewhere. I'll let Virgil explain when we get to the boat."

"And how would this partner feel about your picking up strange men at hotel swimming pools?"

"He's all for it. He's interested in your work and theories. I told you, he's a bit like you."

"You're referring to the Brad Pitt, George Clooney and the other guy thing?"

"No, I mean he's an outsider to academia, like you."

"You really are playing with the devil. What's happened to your academic purity?"

She shrugged. "Sometimes things come along in life to change you."

Was she referring to *retinitis pigmentosa*? Or to something else?

"And of course, there's your assistant tagging along," I said.

"Saneya, yes. She's an Egyptology student."

I turned to look up at the long veranda of the hotel. I saw the Egyptian female assistant I'd met her earlier and she gave me a cheery wave.

Someone else was watching from the hotel's veranda. I glimpsed a young man further along the veranda, training binoculars on us. The man turned aside at my glance, shifting his inspection to the river, where feluccas sliced white wedges in the blue waters of Aswan. This woman who once gazed down on Egypt from the perspective of outer space and now taps the ground with a stick intrigues me.

Yes there is an irony about the distribution of afflictions, which troubles me a little about God's sense of humour. Dr Constance Somers, space archaeologist, goes blind. Beethoven goes deaf. The actor who played Superman, the superhero who leaps tall buildings at a single bound, ends up in an iron lung. Physicist Stephen Hawkings with his sprawling universe of a mind ends up trapped in a twisted body in a wheelchair. The perfect being, Jesus, ends up nailed to a wooden cross. What ironic twist is waiting for me? An alternative Egyptologist who has a mind crammed with arcane information about the religion, magic and funerary practices of a forgotten civilization ends up with amnesia or dementia and forgets ancient Egypt entirely?

Feluccas cut white wedges in the Nile

The Egyptologist with a wand

I feel a current of history swirling around Philae Temple

This morning we took a small boat to the Temple of Philae, clusters of temple buildings nestling foetus-like amid the waters of Lake Nasser, beneath a cobalt sky. We crossed the temple courtyard lined by serried shadows of columns in porticoes and overlooked by the soaring pylons of Philae temple.

We reached a small structure on the northern end of the colonnade, in front of the main temple of Isis.

"And here stands the chapel of Imhotep," she said as if she were the guide.

"You don't need me," I said. "Is that stick in your hand a wand?"

Constance had insisted on walking on her own, her long cane held out ahead of her, sweeping and tapping.

But then she probably knows this place better than I do. She carries her cane like an ancient Egyptian with a staff of office and advances with a confident, even presiding air that is light years away from evoking pity. As before, she hid her blindness behind silvery dark glasses and today dressed casually in a T-shirt and khaki cargo pants. Her assistant, the Egyptian girl Saneya, heavily wrapped and covered in a headscarf, strolled behind, carrying a pink parasol, a curious affectation for a local, but it added a dreamlike timelessness to our progress through the site.

A young man watched from the shadows

"This late period chapel is of course just a shell now," I said, "but the legacy of the man it's dedicated to, a commoner elevated to a god, fills every corner of Egypt, don't you agree?"

"Imhotep. What do you make of him, Anson? Virgil believes there was something a bit alien about him."

We entered the chapel and I continued: "The ancients certainly thought of him as an unearthly individual and worthy of elevating to a god. Here on the forecourt walls are images of the king, Ptolemy the Fourth, paying homage to him, along with a collegiate group of gods, including Osiris, Knum, Sater, Anukis and Isis. He's in powerful company. Imhotep holds in his hand a long white cane... did I say cane? I meant of course his long, thin staff of office and power. As with Joseph, all of Egypt bent under the rod of Imhotep, the most powerful man after pharaoh, extending him the unheard of honour of having his name written at the base of the king's statues, in his role as Overseer of Works. With his luminous intelligence, Imhotep must have seemed like a being that dropped out of the sky to early generations... designer and builder of the first great monument in stone, the step pyramid, deified after his death and revered by the later Greeks and Romans. All this and Imhotep fathered medicine, was considered a wizard, governed as Vizier and held high sacred office. But an ancient alien in Egypt? No, that's a bit fringe even for me. Shall we go around the temple first? There's something I'd like to look for."

We passed the main temple of Isis, pylon planes of stone in blazing sun and walked down the side of the building. The soaring stone stood like a fortress to pagan deity. But it had failed in the end to protect Isis and the rest of the pantheon.

"I always feel a current of history swirling around the Temple of

Philae," I went on, "even though the whole temple has been moved from its original island to this one to save it from the horror of the Aswan dam. I think about how

these temple stones have been flooded by more than
Nile waters over thousands of years, but also by the
arrival of Roman Christianity that swept away the old
religion and ritual and even took away the old language.
The last ancient ceremony of the old religion took place
here in this precinct, the last chant of the priests, the
last rattle of the priestesses' sistra – the last rattle of a
dying civilization you might say - and the last
hieroglyphic texts ever written were carved on these
walls. I imagine the last moment, when a stone mason
cut the very last glyph and then the chisel fell silent and
so did Egypt."

"Egypt's none too silent today," she said as an Egyptian
guide went by, spraying a commentary in Italian at a
group of tourists who seemed to pay scant attention.

"Let's stop here a while," I said.

We were at the rear of the temple.

"What is it you wanted to see?" Dr Constance Somers
said.

"The remains of a low wall behind the temple, part of a
perambulatory," I said. "The wall is broken off after a
few courses of stone and reveals the remaining legs and
feet of a goddess, cut off above the knees."

"Yes, I know it."

The last hieroglyphic texts were carved on these walls

"But here's what's interesting. The sun from the temple roof casts a line of shadow from the temple just beneath the feet of the goddess, creating a sacred, liminal moment as the goddess stands on a threshold between darkness and light, perhaps the darkness of death and the light of eternity..."

"You don't disappoint."

"It's almost at the exact point now."

"Where is the line? Can you show me?" She held out her hand.

A swarthy young visitor further down the wall turned to look at us as I placed her hand on the stone.

"I'm glad one of us is an accredited Egyptologist," I said in a low voice, "or what we're doing could be frowned upon."

"I don't think it's going to bother anyone. Vision impaired tourists are allowed to touch granite and alabaster pieces in the Cairo museum," she said. She ran her fingertips beneath the feet of the goddess.

"Sun warmed stone," she said. "I love the way the sun brings life each day to cold, dead history."

She stands on a threshold between darkness and light

"Wait for it. You're about to join her in her divine omnipresence, existing in the real world and in the divine. Here it comes. There! Do you feel it?"

"I do. Yes, as clearly as if I can see it."

"Can you see anything?" I said.

She tilted her head. "I see two bands, brilliance and darkness and the edges blurred. Ironic. That's my situation exactly. I'm standing on the edge of light and darkness. And yes, I can just make out two shapes like wedges here, her feet?"

"Yes. Like all goddesses she is shown with slender, long feet to increase their divine connection with the ground.

 "Shall we go inside the main temple now?" she said.

We turned to retrace our steps. I took her arm to guide her, but she shook her head.

"No thanks. Let me try. It's a good test of my memory and my cane skills."

"Are you sure? The temple stones can be uneven."

"As I've learnt painfully! I kept stubbing my toes. So I've stopped wearing open sandals in Egypt as my sight has deteriorated."

"Doctor Somers is a very independent lady," the Egyptian girl Saneya said with a chuckle.

"So I am learning."

I mustn't underestimate the Egyptologist. She is surprisingly capable.

Although I know Philae well, I cannot imagine getting around the place with my eyes shut, yet Constance clearly holds a plan of the site in her mind.

I fell in with her, watching her make use of the tip of the cane to probe ahead.

"You're brave about your condition."

"Not brave. Just grimly determined. I spent my life pursuing the illumination of scholarship, and then this happened. Now I have a hunger to find the light of a different, more lasting kind."

What light?

Religious belief? Emotional fulfilment?

"Don't brush aside your achievements," I said. "You've made great discoveries, including that stela of Prince Khaemwaset, who is a pet subject of mine."

"A confession. I can't take all the credit for my finds. Even before I started losing my sight I was using visual aids. Satellite technology. My four-hundred-kilometre-long white cane in the sky. It did most of the work for me. That and a lot of backroom analysis using infra red and colour coding to map and locate buried sites. I have spent my life seeing beyond the visible light spectrum. It's a twist of fate that once, using images from outer space, I was able to scan areas under the ground as small as a dinner plate and now I can't see the flag stones under my feet!"

"Was there something you were working on when your condition grew worse?"

She was silent for a time.

"You're a perceptive man, but don't ask me that. Not yet. Just concentrate on being my eyes in Egypt. I'm enjoying it, hearing your voice and, picturing the Egypt of your perceptions. It's a good thing you are murmuring to me though or authorities might think you're giving a commentary on site and you're not a registered Egyptian guide. Foreign guides are not permitted as I'm sure you know, and normally save their descriptions for when they're back on the cruise boat."

Our cruise boat lies berthed at Aswan, awaiting our return, an antique and elegant *dahabeeyah* yacht, filled with modern luxury and Arabesque adornments and fitted with cabins for a select group of fourteen passengers. I have yet to meet them, including her partner, who is due to arrive from the United States.

"We see images of Isis carved on the pylon," I said.

"Along with her son Horus. The serpentine form of the goddess in her tight sheath dress turns the bright stone smooth and sensuous. The associations of snakes and ancient Egyptian femininity found their apotheosis in Cleopatra and her asp."

"Serpentine goddesses. A weakness perhaps?" she said. We moved on towards the temple doorway.

I noticed a young man standing as immobile as the columns that flanked him, watching us from the shadows. How had he got there so fast? It was the same young man who had been standing at the rear of the temple.

Isis on the pylon

Solidly built, swarthy, good-looking. Noticing my glance, he detached himself from the shadows and walked away. He had a pair of binoculars on a strap around his neck.

We filed out of the small, darkened sanctuary of Isis. Saneya had been last to go in and so she left the cloistered area first, followed by Constance, and I brought up the rear.

I paused at the doorway and swept a last look around the chamber at the walls showing reliefs of Isis cast in a greenish glow from the strip lights on the floor. Sad that Constance couldn't see the patina of mystery that clung to the rippled forms of Isis, but I had tried to give her a sense of the numinous in this shrine that lay nestled at the heart of Philae.

I heard their footsteps retreating and went out after them.

That's when I stepped straight into that meaty hand that clamped around my mouth and I was hauled off bodily to a darker side chamber.

Who were the two young men in the temple this morning?

Spy satellite people? Agents of the secretive US National Reconnaissance Office? They didn't actually say so. And why are they suddenly taking an interest in the work of the blind space archaeologist? Did she make a discovery in her satellite archaeology that has global security ramifications?

I caught up with the two women outside the temple, walking across the clearing to the structure known as the Kiosk of Trajan.

Once the main entrance to the temple from the river, its screened columns rise high into the sky supporting the architraves.

The locals call the place Pharaoh's Bed. A fourteen poster.

"I have an excuse for getting lost," Constance said.

"What's yours? I was about to send Saneya back to look for you."

"Just a guy in there trying to pick my brains."

"A guy?"

Caution advised me against lying to her.

How quickly do people who have lost their sight start to sharpen their remaining senses, especially hearing? Is there a swift compensation by the body and brain? Can a blind person's ears pick up and distinguish between the sounds of movement of two people instead of just one?

Hauled off bodily into a darker side chamber

"Two guys, as a matter of fact. I suggested they hire their own guide."

If the two NRO men are telling the truth, then what kind of site has Dr Constance entered - with impunity - while it is deadly to others?

I watched her with even more respect as she stepped inside the screened columns of the Kiosk of Trajan, sweeping her wand ahead of her. Surely she is more vulnerable than anyone, or is her lack of vision a protection against something that others see?

Nile currents

View from our dahabeeyah

Back in my well-appointed cabin on the boat, I sit back on my double bed with a riverside view. I can see the Tombs of the Nomarchs, little puncture holes in eternity, the sweep of the stairs going up and the mausoleum of the Aga Khan perched on top, Islam asserting itself over ancient Egypt. The two are forever in tension.

We hear of a clash of civilizations between Islam and the West.

But there has long been a clash of civilizations going on right here for centuries and I wonder which one is going to be the winner five centuries from now. I think I know. Will we all be robbed of ancient Egypt one day, just as Constance has been robbed of it by losing her sight? I can't imagine the loss I would feel if I could never see the remains of Egypt again, here on the banks of River Nile, the world's largest museum.

Yet blindness and ancient Egypt have a long association.

Blind musicians were a tradition

Many of the tombs of Egypt, such as the tomb of the vizier Nacht, show blind musicians. Blind musician were a tradition and certainly preferable in a pharaoh's House of the Secluded, or harem.

We imagine a blind musician singing the song of the harper:

I have heard the words of Imhotep and Hordjedef,
Whose sayings are recited in whole.
What of their places?
Their walls have crumbled,
Their places are gone,
As though they had never been!
None comes from there,
To tell us how they fare,
To calm our hearts,
Until we go to the place where they have gone!

The transcripts of The Rameses Harem Conspiracy tell us that a blind harem steward Paibekkamen, 'the Blind One', was at the heart a plot to murder the king. I imagine the blind steward listening to the whispered secrets of the royals in the harem, pulling on invisible strings as he orchestrates a conspiracy from within his world of shadows.

I feel glad to be on the Nile again. I recall that Mother
Nile floated the baby Moses snugly in his basket and the
river always floats my boat. On the Nile I feel I am part
of the current of time and history. On this great river
flowing out of deepest Africa, Cleopatra once floated, her
perfumed sails making the winds drunk, as
Shakespeare tells us. What's not to love?
But my boat is rocking a little as I think about my
abduction today. The current is gathering speed and
force and I'm starting to think that this may not be the
leisurely Nile interlude that Constance suggested
to me.
Constance has been working in Saqqara and so I go
online, looking at Lower Egypt and the River Nile from
space.

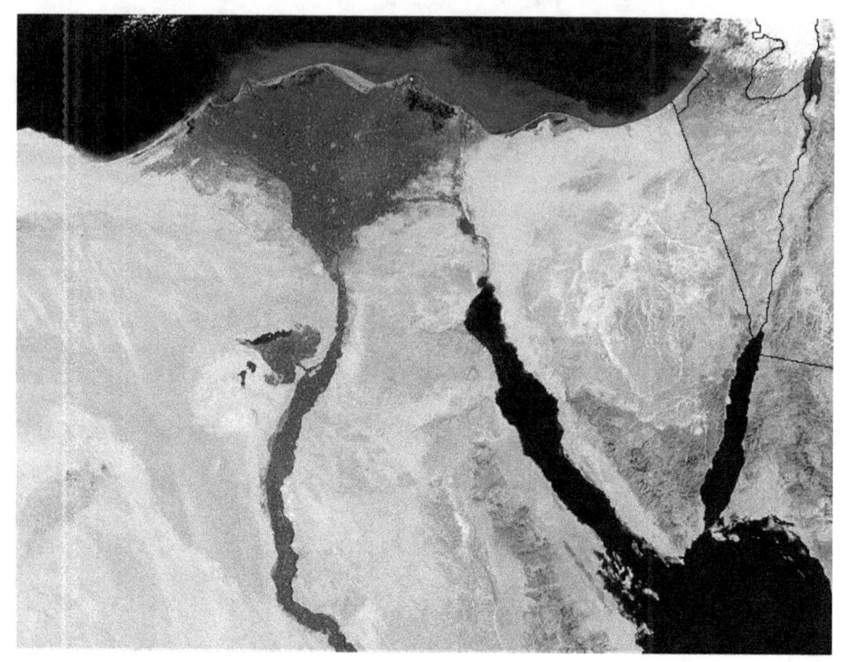

Nile Delta. Wikipedia

It looks faintly erotic from a satellite. Is it just me?
Maybe Constance is getting to me. Or maybe Constance
is right. I am preoccupied with the pervasive feminine in
ancient Egypt… Isis, Hathor, Seshat… and all of those
slinky goddesses who bring the walls of ancient Egypt
sinuously to life.

I recall Constance's words: "I'm no lady. I don't want
censorship, be warned. I want your sensual reactions,
too. I know you feel a powerful attraction to the feminine
allure of ancient Egypt, so if something turns you on,
turn me on!"

The pervasive feminine in ancient Egypt

She is intriguing, this woman who lives in dark mystery.
What are her secrets?

Constance has been working in Saqqara, so I go to
Google maps and look at space images of Saqqara. I see
a shot of a rumpled sheet, creased with dents, squares
and shadows. Thousand of eyes have pored over shots
like these. Before she lost her sight, did Constance see
something here that others didn't? She must have lost a

very good pair of eyes, because I can't see what has stirred up US Intelligence.

Saqqara, Google maps

The UFOlogist on the Nile

Today I met 'the partner'. Virgil Powell is a tall, aquiline man with a stony face and lengthy hair combed back from a high forehead.

He came up the gangplank of our twin-masted, one hundred foot *dahabeeyah* Ayesha with a measured step, like a wading bird, a loose coat fluttering like a cape in a breeze, a steward in tow with his bags. I thought immediately of an ibis.

He has the same hard yet hopeful gleam in the eye that I have seen in those opportunistic birds.

Imhotep was also called the son of the creator god Ptah

Constance introduced us and he grappled my hand. "You're our man, Anson," he said. He was a little older than me. "Just the one to help bring the light to Constance, and reveal not just what's there, that everyone can see, but what lies hidden beneath the surface of Egypt, the unknown."

"I'll try."

"Good man, and right now, my eyes have spotted the fact that the bar is open. A drink should wash away my jet lag."

The steward went off with his bag to a cabin and Constance allowed Powell to take her arm and I followed the pair across the polished wooden deck to a spread of low Arabesque divans at the rear of the private yacht. Saneya, the assistant, was nowhere to be seen. Maybe she was in the shade somewhere, avoiding the long rays of sunset.

Evidently she is the opposite of her sun-worshipping ancient sisters and seems to prefer the protection of verandas, heavy dress, parasols and cabins.

We sat down and a drinks steward took our orders.

"Love this twenties nostalgia stuff," Powell said, looking around at the boat. "It was an age that still believed in romance and wonder, the age of Sherlock Holmes and

the Tutankhamun discovery, the sensational curse, and
so on and so forth."
"I warned Anson that your interests are outside of the
conventional."
The bird-like eyes in the cultivated face settled on me.
"I'm a
paranormalist. My specialty is ufology, paranormal
phenomena and so on. There are many convinced about
Egypt's links with the stars."
"I'm one of them. The ancients observed the stars
assiduously and it regulated their calendar."
"No, I'm suggesting that it was a two-way affair."
"You mean aliens built the pyramids, that kind of
thing?"
Powell allowed a flicker of a smile to soften his features.
"Answer me this. The genius who designed the very first
pyramid,
Imhotep, the father of medicine and of writing as well as
being the
High Priest... where do you imagine he came from?"
I have always been in awe of the genius and polymath,
architect and inventor of the first great buildings in
stone, whose fame preceded and overshadowed
Leonardo da Vinci's, but my reverence stops short of
Powell's implication.

"Ankhtowe, a suburb of Memphis. His father was Kanofer, a master builder, and his mother, Khredu-ankh, came from the Mendes area…"

"A later accretion. It was also said that Imhotep's father was the creator god Ptah and his mother was the sky goddess Nut. Some are convinced that Imhotep was the original ancient alien. Don't you think that there is something a bit alien about the imp-like figures of Imhotep in the world's museums, showing him as a tiny sage seated on a chair with a scroll across his knee and his elongated skull extruded inside a skullcap? Then there is the curious meaning of his name.

Imhotep means 'The one who comes in peace.' Isn't that canonically the message communicated by friendly, and sometimes deceptive, visitors from the stars, in countless science fiction stories and movies… 'we come in peace'?"

I have met UFOlogists before, people who believe that extra terrestrials are the secret accelerants of human development. But this revelation heightens my curiosity.

The imp-like polymath who preceded Leonardo da Vinci

The UFOlogist – satellite space archaeology – The U.S. National

Reconnaissance Office… carriages in a train of associations slam together in my mind.

Just what has Constance found?

I recall the warning given by the NRO twins: "Dr Somers has attracted the interest of groups that want to discover what she knows."

Does Virgil Powell belong to one of these groups?

Our drinks arrived and I sipped a whisky and soda.

I wonder about her attraction to this man. Maybe it's the voice. Rich, enveloping, it would wrap around her and give her a sense of comfort.

Has he ingratiated himself with the blind Egyptologist to serve his own ends?

"You believe in UFOs?" Powell said to me, over his gin and tonic.

"I'm sure there are thousands of unidentified flying objects spotted in the skies each year."

"Yes, but alien ones."

"Do I believe that extra-terrestrials came all the way to ancient Egypt to help build something as useful as pyramids? No. Do you believe in flying saucers?"

"The sightings speak for themselves. I was formerly a NASA official, before heading up my satellite communication organisation. We all knew of strange occurrences."

"But what exactly are they? I take an interest in the esoteric and in unknown dangers and I've learnt that wherever there is documented UFO activity, it's invariably accompanied by paranormal activity, ghostly sighting and supernatural phenomena, which may be described as demonic in nature. So should humankind be worrying about an alien invasion, or a demonic invasion, instead?”

The intense and imposing man looked dubious.

“Some make the link between ufology and demonology. The Internet is full of it. But they are two very different concepts to hold in your head at the same time. The first, demonic, requires a belief in the opposite, a god. The second, nuts and bolts flying saucers, requires an atheistic view of the universe, unless you are that horrible contradiction, a Biblical UFOlogist, one who believes aliens visited earth in chariots of fire as instruments of god’s purpose – angelic astronauts.”

“So you’re betting on the nuts and bolts variety?”

“I wait and watch with fearful and fearsome interest for the truth to be revealed to the world. And you? Do you believe in a god, Anson? It’s odd how people often suggest that god or Jesus were ancient astronauts, yet few suggest that the devil, Lucifer, may have been exactly that, since we are expressly told that he fell from heaven.”

“To answer your question,” I said, “my belief system is an eternal tension of opposites, light and dark, good and evil, rational and magic.”

In the dark with a blind Egyptologist

The climb up sweeping steps to the tombs

This afternoon we climbed the caramel-coloured cliffs overlooking the Nile and the town of Aswan.

We visited tombs of the Old Kingdom Nomarchs, ancient governors of he region, reached after a long climb up a sweeping flight of sand-strewn steps.

We paused outside a text-covered façade in granite that gave off a crystalline glare in the late morning. It was the tomb of Harkhuf, a famous Nomarch.

"Do you want me to talk about the records written on here," I said to her. "About the letter from Pharaoh Pepy to the tomb owner, carved on the wall? Or maybe the story of the expedition into Africa where Harkhuf returns with a dancing pygmy to delight the heart of the boy king? No? Then how about Harkhuf's curse? There's an impressive one on his tomb: 'As for any man who enters this tomb as if it were his own, I shall seize his neck like that of a duck or goose and, for that, he shall be judged by the Great God.' And over here beside the doorway, stands an image of the ancient worthy himself, holding a long staff in his hand exactly like your long cane. Shall we go inside?"

"Not this one. Let's go to the deeper tomb of Mekhu and Sabni.' She spoke quietly to her assistant, Saneya. "Wait for us outside the entrance, Saneya, and keep the guard occupied. Give me a call if anyone else shows up."

We moved on to the tomb of the governor Mekhu and his son Sabni.

I continued: "I always feel guilty passing by a tomb without responding to the tomb owners request: O, you living who are upon the earth and who pass before this tomb, whether going upstream or downstream on the river, say these words - 'may a thousand loaves and a thousand pots of beer belong to the owner of this tomb' There, I've said it."

Only the three of us made the visit to the necropolis of cliff side tombs today, our last excursion before the boat sets sail for Luxor. Virgil Powell skipped the tour, preferring to remain on board and 'kick-back' following his long journey from the United States.

The light dimmed as we entered the column-filled tomb cut into the cliff.

There is no lighting in these tombs, or, if there is a lighting system, it was not in operation today.

I felt in a pocket for a flashlight.

"No, don't. Let's be in darkness. It puts us on an equal footing."

"Me on an equal footing with an academic? That's novel."

"You can hold my arm."

I took her elbow lightly. "I'll try not to bump you into a column."

"I'm thinking about your safety."

The blind young woman led me deeper into warm, dusty gloom, split by pale columns that were soon swallowed by darkness. She guided me, tapping the columns and the floor, taking me through an echoing hall, and then proceeding into the sanctuary of the tomb owner's son.

"What do you think of me?" she said.

"I'm pretty much in the dark about you, literally. I know you're a university professor who has teamed up with a very weird UFOlogist."

I also know something else.

She is the subject of a secret investigation and I am now part of it, carrying that little tracking device around with me in my pocket. I imagine it beeping somewhere and being watched by a pair of curious eyes. Or maybe two pairs of eyes. The mysterious twins.

Instead of mentioning that, I said: "What's going on there with the UFOlogist? You're partners – in what sense? Do you suppose he's befriended you because he wants something?"

"Don't you think he might find me personally attractive? Some men can see past the poor blind girl with the white cane thing."

"I know I do."

"Prove it to me."

"How?"

"Now."

"Really?"

The blind young woman led me deeper

I heard a clatter as her cane fell to the stone floor.

That's surprising. The pale white strip is her lifeline and she just dropped it. That's an emphatic act of abandon. Now she drew closer, so that I could hear her breathing. "Don't move." Her fingers found my face in the blackness. Soft, perfumed tips. As she had done once before, she explored my face as though she wanted to read me like Braille.

"I like you, Anson." Her voice, in deep darkness, without the accompanying vision of her, was deeply intimate. Her words seemed to curl in my ears.

God, why do we men always want the lights switched on? She knows something about darkness.

She came closer and surprisingly kissed my lips.

I kissed her in willing return.

Of course, in my mind, I did much more and much more occurred… I saw it all happen in a flash that lit up the darkness.

"Let's really be equal," she said.

"What did you have in mind?"

She undid the top button of my shirt.

"This is never going to make us equal," I said, "but it might reveal some delightful differences."

I took over from her and undid my shirt and the rest and I heard the rustle of her clothing and after a moment there was an electric silence before we touched and found each other's warmth. "Wait." She wanted to resume her fingertip examination of me and this time it was a wide ranging field survey in granular darkness, starting from my shoulders and running across my chest and tickling down my belly. I shuddered as she sheathed me inside her fingers, feathery light fingers that explored me.

"You were right, there is more of you."

We undressed and sank to the floor on our clothes and I stretched over her and it was she who guided me into another, deeper, softer darkness, except instead of

darkness I found dancing lights that played down my
spine and my legs and inside my head.
Why do they call lust blind?
This was visionary, galaxy-probing sex.
She squirmed and kissed my neck over and over and I
felt the warm humidity of her breath in my nape.
A great light came from a distance.
See the light. See it!
It slowly rose to an explosion of brilliance. When the
brilliance exploded, it spread out in tingles of after-lights
throughout my body.
Was that the kind of light she was seeking so hungrily in
her life?

"You asked me a question before," she said. "I think I've answered it. I like Virgil, but I don't belong to him. He's an intriguing man. An expert with arcane knowledge, like you. I get lonely in my shrinking world. I imagined kissing you that day we met in the gardened pool of the Cataract hotel."

"But why hook up with a flying saucer crank like him, not to mention an alternative Egyptologist like me? We're both highly questionable."

"Because you both hold keys to doors that I need to open. One has the key to other worlds, alien worlds. The other has a key to unlock the barriers that may stand in my way. Help me reach the light I want to find. I need you, especially you. I know you have a unique knowledge of ancient Egyptian religion and funerary practices that mainstream Egyptologists shy away from. You also have a notorious ability to penetrate the most impenetrable of tombs and sanctuaries to reach the secrets of the ancients."

"You need me, yet you're locking away some dark secret in your inner world and you won't trust me enough to tell me."

"I want you to be patient. I cannot say anything yet, not to you, and especially not to the Egyptian authorities and the archaeological establishment."

That explained why she was dealing with outsiders.

She picked up her cane and we left the tomb. I walked out with a newborn wonder for this woman who carried a wand. I also felt a wave of protectiveness, and anxiety. A blind young space archaeologist was the focal point of some murky conspiracy in Egypt and I was starting to care about her.

Me and a blind girl?

Why not?

Love is blind and I quite like the unconventionality of it.

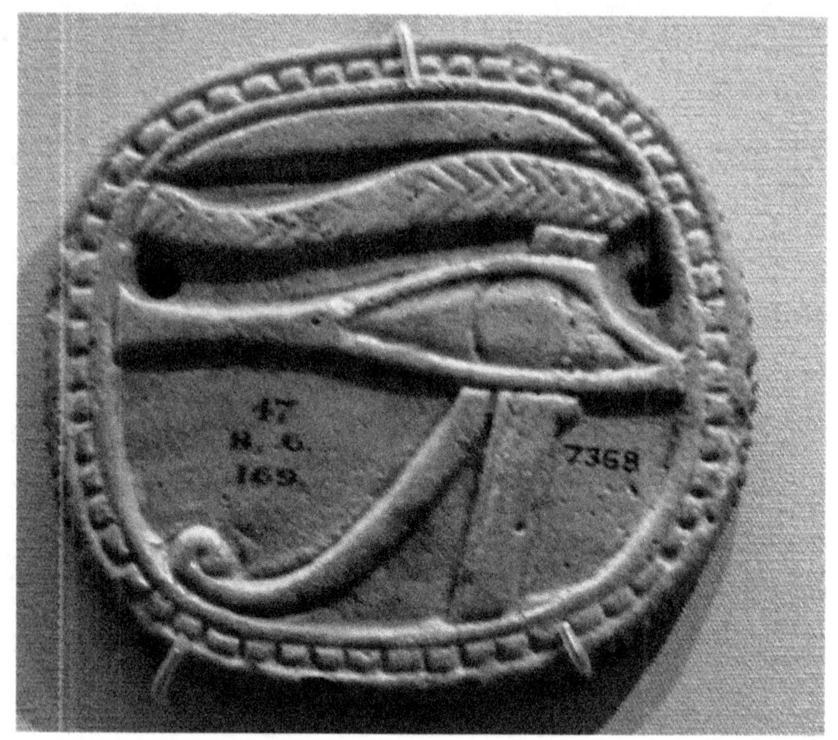

Focal point of a conspiracy in Egypt

I've spent my life looking for the unseen mysteries of ancient Egypt and she has spent hers searching beyond the visible light spectrum through her satellite archaeology.

Maybe we belong together. It could be a very agreeable, symbiotic arrangement.

Like the words of the song, 'I only have eyes for you'.

And she could only have ears for me.

This union between alternative and mainstream Egyptology could help bridge the growing alienation of the two sides.

I came up on deck after a long and pleasantly reflective shower in my cabin to find we were on the move. *Ayesha* had shaken free of her moorings at Aswan and changed into a living thing, fluttering and creaking under canvas and ropes and she was cutting serenely through the shimmer of the Nile.

Feluccas under sail, as well as riverbanks lined with stands of palms, slid by and the gentle breeze brought coolness to the afternoon.

Virgil Powell was sitting on a divan at the rear of the antique yacht, an iPad on his lap.

A few other passengers were stretched out on loungers, enjoying drinks served by Egyptian stewards in attendance.

"Did Constance enjoy the sights, as seen through your eyes?" he said.

"I'm hoping so."

The hard yet hopeful eyes of the older man turned briefly hard.

"There's something you should remember about Constance. She's a scientist, first and foremost, and her science is archaeological exploration. She has a tendency to see people as tools to her ends, like satellite imagery or an archaeological shovel."

He was not a man to be underestimated.

"How did you meet her?"

"You're guessing Constance and I don't move in the same circles and you're right. But I was in the field of satellite technology and I was attended one of her public lectures on space archaeology and fell under her spell."

I sat nearby.

"Was she blind at that stage?"

Powell softened enough to crack a joke.

"You're thinking she must have been blind to hook up with me?'

"No, I'm just wondering how a blind archaeologist gives a lecture on space archaeology. It's a pretty visual subject, I'd have thought."

"She had a visual aid."

"Besides her cane."

"Saneya. Her protégé. Although she's still a student, Saneya probably knows as much about space archaeology as any other Egyptian or American Egyptologist."

There I go underestimating people again. The Egyptian girl who hides herself under wraps is also hiding special qualifications.

"Were you hoping her satellite work might locate ancient aliens?"

"Visitors have been here in Egypt's ancient past and the evidence of them is still around today. Have you seen those mysterious images under a lintel in the temple of Seti at Abydos, including a flying disk-shaped craft, a helicopter, a hover craft and so on and so forth?"

"Yes, and also what appears to be a military tank," I said. "But I wonder why the aliens would trundle out World War Two mechanised warfare against people with swords, spears, bows and arrows."

The mysterious images in the temple of Seti

"If you have a better explanation, apart from the one of freakish and highly selective weathering and deterioration, which so-called experts offer, I'd like to hear it."

 I shrugged.

"Maybe you're right, Virgil, and maybe all of Egyptology is wrong. If space archaeologists like Constance can discover scores of lost pyramids, maybe the technology can also detect a crashed mother ship from another galaxy, buried under the sands."

His eyes glinted.

"There had to be a reason for the Egyptians' obsession with the stars, a powerful reason why they oriented pyramids to the belt of Orion and the circumpolar stars and so on. Aren't we told that when pharaoh died he joined the imperishable stars, that pharaoh's Boat of

Millions of Years travelled through the star-lined body of the sky goddess Nut?"

"You believe Constance found your evidence?"

"You won't get an answer from me on that. You'll have to ask her."

Constance is not entirely independent, I have found, especially at meal times.

Tonight we had a buffet dinner by lamplight on deck and while Virgil Powell was caught up in a discussion with a retired bishop who had religious views of ancient Egyptian history, I decided to help out.

"While those two are locked in mortal conversation, shall I serve you dinner? What do you fancy?"

"Surprise me."

I joined the growing line of passengers being served by a white-jacketed Egyptian waiter.

I brought our two meals back to the table and put hers in front of her.

"While I like surprises," she said, "I like to know what's in front of me. Can you give me an aerial survey?"

"Honeyed barbecued duck in the ancient Egyptian style at twelve o'clock. Spicy lamb kofta, three o'clock. Fava beans at six, spreading to nine, with char-grilled eggplant in the middle of the clock face..."

"Thank you. A very clear satellite report."

The bishop, an amateur Biblical archaeologist, was making the case that Imhotep and Joseph could have been one and the same person.

I know the argument.

There is a stela right here on a rock in Aswan, known as the Famine Stela, and it tells of a seven year famine in the reign of the pharaoh Djoser that Imhotep brought to an end. The story of drought and famine also involves the king having a dream where the god spoke to him about the rise of the Nile and the end of the drought.

Aswan Famine Stela Wikipedia

"What do you think about all of this, Anson?" the fragile old Bishop said.

I shrugged.

"Seven year cycles of drought were common in Egypt. I find it interesting that in the Bible, Joseph is said to have come up with the idea of taxing the people grain to build up reserves for hard times. Paying taxes in kind was always the way of Egypt from the year dot and so that bit of the story hardly fits the chronology of Joseph."

"So the chronology is wrong and that puts Joseph in a much earlier time frame – the age of Djoser and Imhotep."

"I doubt that," the UFOlogist said. "And I don't think Imhotep was put here by any Hebrew god." Powell turned his eyes up to the sky of stars above our boat. "Maybe he was sent from one of those stars, yes."

"Religion at dinner seems impossible to avoid in Egypt," Constance said to me. "But then I suppose it's impossible to think of ancient Egypt without religion. I think that's what I loved about satellite archaeology. It seemed that I was above the clouds of religion, including the ancient Egyptian kind, Christianity and Islam."

Imhotep's dark agenda

Temple of Kom Ombo

This morning our vessel *Ayesha* stopped at the temple of Kom Ombo.

"I want to show *you* something," she said. "Something that's not quite what it appears to be." Questing ahead of herself like an eager insect with a feeler, Constance led our group to a wall outside the temple of Kom Ombo, a large Ptolemaic temple with hypostyle halls, set on a hill near a bend in the Nile. She took us to a wall behind the temple. It's a famous scene. Carefully laid out in the Egyptian manner is a display of surgical instruments that any surgeon today will instantly recognise. Forceps, scalpels, probes, saw blades, scales, scissors, hooks, cupping vessels, a dilator, catheter, rows of flasks, even prescriptions. They're all spread out before an image of the seated god of medicine Imhotep.

Constance stopped in front of the display and ran her hands, oddly unsteady, over the tools.

"These instruments intrigue me," she said.

"They make me wince," I said. "A pretty excruciating display, I always think. But it shows the astonishing level of medical science in ancient times. Further along there's an instrument that looks uncannily like a stethoscope, along with twin cords for the physician's ears and a cup to put on the patient's chest. And the stethoscope was supposed to have been invented by a Frenchman in the nineteenth century."

"Yes, but why did such a great advance in science suddenly occur?" she said.

"I hope you're not going to give more oxygen to the aliens theory."

Surgical instruments that any surgeon today will instantly recognise

"It was all given to Egypt by the father of medicine, Imhotep," she said. "That's why there's a carving of him right here beside the tools he invented. But think about it. Isn't it curious that surgery and medicine came to flower just as Egypt embarked on its first great national works, the construction of the step pyramid, involving thousands of workers? Was Imhotep really a benevolent figure to the world? I'll tell you. He gave Egypt medicine and surgery in order to keep his vast workforce going."

I've never thought of that. She stated it as a matter of fact.

"Just a theory," she said, breaking away from the wall. "Now show me your Kom Ombo."

Kom Ombo hypostyle hall

On the river of time

This afternoon, I came out on deck to find Constance stretched out on a lounger in her black swimming costume, while Saneya sat under the shade of a deck canopy, reading a book. This was how the blind archaeologist had looked when I first met her at Aswan, except today she sat not under the shade of palms, but gently flapping sails.

Nile village

I had brought my MacBook with me.
"Constance. I was just going to sit here and update my Egyptology blog, but I'd much rather talk to you."

"Come here and read to me instead. What are you writing about? Is it your latest theory? You never told me why you were in Aswan."

"I came here on the trail of Prince Khaemwaset. There's an Aswan rock, a family stela that shows Rameses, Khaemwaset and his mother, as well as some of the prince's siblings. Khaemwaset is shown with the god Knum, a creator god. I just wonder what the explorative prince was really doing here."

"Did you find out?"

"No. But Khaemwaset always interests me. He identified, visited and labelled more tombs than you've spotted by satellite. I firmly believe he explored Egypt in search of forbidden knowledge."

"We have that in common. I feel I am walking in his footsteps too. Maybe all Egyptologists do."

"You found the prince's stela."

"Yes."

"Does Khaemwaset have anything to do with the secret you're keeping from me?"

"Very astute, but I'm not going to say."

"I asked Virgil if you'd ever found evidence of his theories in your satellite work."

"What did he say?"

"He said to ask you."

"Let's not talk about my work. Let's talk about yours. Read me one of your Egypt blogs. Something mysterious about dangers from the ancient past."

"Okay. Here's one. It's a reflection on Egypt's forbidden dangers and it relates to my own experience of evil."

I read from the blog.

I've never seen my lifelong pursuit of ancient Egypt as inviting an encounter with unseen forces... and yet...

I believe in dangers from the ancient past.

And perhaps it's no wonder these and other 'self-destructive' notions and theories make me an outsider in my profession.

On two separate occasions in my life I've experienced the shattering impact of a *mysterium tremendum* and it's not something that I can easily bring myself to admit.

The episodes were embarrassingly spiritualist in nature. I wrestle with a faith and I call myself an Anglican, but God probably wouldn't agree.

These events occurred, not in one of my many visits to Egypt, nor in a tomb or temple, but while asleep in my bed in my Oxford apartment.

I had surfaced from deep sleep to feel my body shaking violently as something descended onto my back and slammed me to the mattress.

The presence paralysed me, pinning me down, like the crushing effects of an anaesthetic.

It welded itself to my spine and to the back of my head like an alien predator in a movie. It felt like a shadow, even though I could not see it. Whatever it was, it did not speak, yet it seemed to be clinging to the back of my brain where it waited and watched as patiently as a parasite.

I could not cry out nor could I break its frightening, determined hold. Something, I knew, was trying to take over me.

What was this terrifying ambush?

Night paralysis?

Or was it the attack of some elemental?

Thoughts of Egypt came into my mind and I wondered - has my obsession opened the door to this? I've given years to the study of Egypt's mystery, and am I now being asked to give more, my very being? How could I shake myself free when every muscle lay paralysed? I didn't know where to go to escape it.

I tried to will the paralysis away with the power of my mind, hoping to break its hold with the force of concentration. I was cold and yet sweated. It would not move and neither could I move.

Its breath lay on my neck and remained there.

It's watching my struggle, I thought. No worse, smiling, demon-like.

Prayer. There was nothing else. I fled to the refuge of an uncertain faith. Christ, help me, I prayed. This, and only this, broke the hold. The shadow finally relaxed its clasp and let go of me, not immediately, but after some moments of thought. It dissolved away. I had passed some kind of test.

Yet it happened again, ten years later, a second attack? Both events left me feeling profoundly shaken and puzzled as well as embarrassed and tinged with guilt. I'd never seen my pursuit of ancient Egypt as an encounter with evil but now I was forced to consider the possibility that some element of it could be hostile to my life and to my wellbeing and might always be waiting...

"Don't tell Virgil that story. He'll call it an alien abduction attempt."

"It was pure evil."

"What do you think would have happened if you'd let go, given in?" she said, as a village on the riverbank slipped past our boat, invisible to her.

"I don't like to think."

"A psychologist might say you are holding back from the terror of letting go of your old fashioned beliefs about religion. The biggest surprise is that you cling to any at all, knowing of your experiential approach to the sacred of ancient Egypt.”

“Belief in religion doesn’t banish the idea of evil entities, it confirms their existence.”

“What an amazing contradiction you are, Anson. A phenomenologist who believes in valuing the sacred of ancient Egypt – and also a man of faith.”

At Edfu temple

We skipped the smaller temple of Esna and visited Edfu, the best-preserved temple in Egypt.

Unreasonably, I felt a twinge of jealousy at the quayside, when Powell helped Constance into a black two-seater *caleche* and I was left to climb into the following carriage with Saneya for the short trip by horse-drawn coach through the town to the temple.

The revolution has dented the tourist trade. Fewer visitors than ever make the trip and the horses pulling the carriages look hungrier than usual.

Saneya had screened herself under a sun hat and scarf and her eyes behind dark glasses. I decided to peel back some of the layers.

"I understand you've been hiding your light under a parasol or a scarf or whatever – and that you're actually a student of space archaeology."

She smiled. She had a homely, cheerful face with the luminous dark eyes that were typically Egyptian, but her response took me by surprise.

"Yes, I'm a full-on geek girl, I'm afraid," she said, with a pronounced

American accent. "Egyptian born, but US educated."

"You're the new generation who will inherit the revolution, however it turns out in the end. Tell me, did the looting and general breakdown of order affect your work with Constance at Saqqara?"

Her smile lingered, but I could see a screen drop down behind her eyes.

"We're managing, thank you." She said it politely, but in a way that did nothing to encourage further discussion. She doesn't want to talk about Constance's work. She knows things.

We walked with Constance and her companion Powell in a narrow passageway between Edfu temple and an outer wall on the west side of the complex. The temple of Edfu, with its massive pylons, the highest in Egypt, was built to mark a great mythological battle between the Lord of chaos Seth and the god Horus, and imagery along the wall dramatised this conflict. "These reliefs, as you know Constance, tell of the titanic struggle between good and evil," I said. "Here Horus is shown harpooning the god of chaos who takes the form of a hippopotamus. A puny hippopotamus, if I may say so. The hippopotamus is shown in miniscule scale in the water in relation to the floating figure of Horus on his skiff, a magical safeguard of course to restraint the beast's demonic power. Some say Horus defeated Seth in this battle, other accounts say that this final battle has yet to take place and that when it does, Osiris, god of the underworld, and the entire pantheon, will return to earth. And at the finale to the re-enactment of a religious performance that took place here, the priests would cut up and eat a cake in the shape of a hippo – again, magic designed to control the forces of chaos."

"That's what it's all about to you, Anson, isn't it?" Powell said, listening in. "Good and evil."

Nile scene

A night on the Nile

There was a *tap, tap, tap* on my cabin door tonight and when I opened it a long white stick came in ahead of Constance.

"I was making passes at you all through dinner. Are you blind?" she said.

"I didn't want to antagonize your partner any more. We already had a run-in this evening."

She came inside and I closed the cabin door behind her.

"That's hardly surprising when you suggested to him that extra-terrestrial intelligence was an over-claim and that aliens must be morons to keep coming all this way just to support the New Age movement."

"Won't you be missed?"

"Don't worry, he's on a conference call, trouble-shooting over some satellite hiccup. He'll be hours."

"Then so will we. Interesting that you both have a space orientation and yet neither of you look heavenward. Two cheerful pagans, it appears, except neither of you are particularly cheerful, especially him."

"Now you want to antagonize me too. If politics and religion should never be discussed over dinner, then the same thing should apply to the bedroom. Where's the bed?"

"Three o'clock."

"Are you going to turn off the lights?"

"God no. But don't worry, I'll keep my eyes tightly shut."

"Did you like what you saw?"

"Yes, I did, and I'm still liking what I see. But now I'm thinking, isn't it a bit late to be keeping secrets from me now that you've shown me so much of you?"

"What secrets?"

"Tell me what you discovered at Saqqara. It's obviously something you've detected through satellite imaging."

"You sound awfully sure about that. Why is that? Have you been talking to someone? I can trust you, can't I?"

I thought of the tracking device sitting in my pocket on the floor of the cabin and felt a twinge of guilt.

I touched her closed eyelids.

"If you've got dark secrets locked behind here then how could anyone else know them to tell me?"

"Be patient a little longer. But now I must go back to my cabin."

"I have finally seen my Dark Lady of the Sonnets, or at least the blonde lady of my onsite commentaries, revealed and in full light.

I feel even more concerned about her. I keep pushing Constance to be honest with me, yet I have not been honest with her. Does she have any idea how many secret eyes are watching her? I picture one of the satellites that provide space archaeology with its infra-red imagery as it rides in space in sun-synchronous orbit above Egypt. It is staring down on Constance, sending down explorative pulses, trying to probe beneath her surface to read her secrets.

From Howard Carter to space archaeology

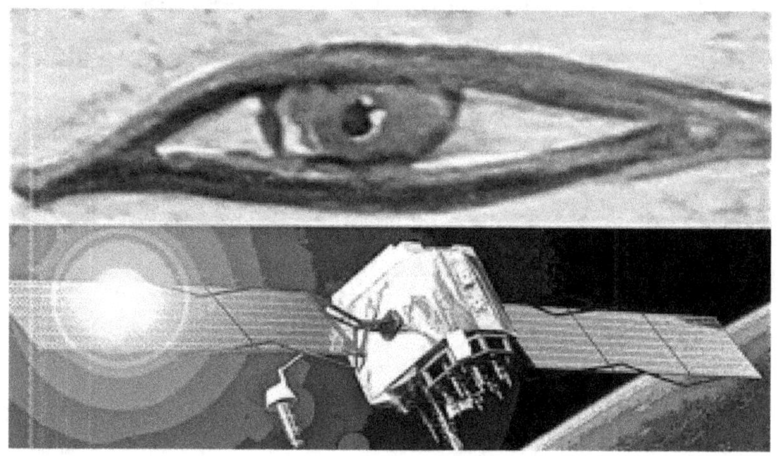

What would Howard Carter make of space archaeology?

Today we disembarked from *Ayesha* and checked into the Winter Palace at Luxor. We plan to base ourselves here for a few days' of exploration before we fly north to Cairo. This afternoon we'll cross to the Valley of the Kings and visit Karnak temple in the morning.

I stretched out my frame on the bed in the Victorian elegance of my room and thought about my surroundings.

Tsars, stars and shahs have all graced this old colonial treasure of a hotel.

Most intriguingly of all, the doyen of Egyptology, Howard Carter, discoverer of the tomb of Tutankhamun, made the announcement to the world of his discovery here. In later years he would sit in the foyer, basking in the fading recognition of guests, a lion of Egyptology reduced to a rather sad, Chaplinesque figure.

Did the Egyptologist ever sleep in this room? I wonder, as I look up at the ceiling. What would Carter have made of this new world of satellite technology? Would he have called it archaeology by proxy?

Howard Carter. Wikipedia

Instead of peering by candlelight through a hole in a wall to view the hoard of treasures inside Tutankhamun's tomb chamber, archaeologists today are

peering down from space to see the treasures below the
sand and in answer to the question "can you see
anything?" they are saying "wonderful things!"
We are finding ancient Egypt from space and there are
those like Virgil
Powell who believe that 'space' found ancient Egypt in
the form of visitors who left their footprints in the
amazing knowledge and technology of a lost
civilization...

Danger from the past

Valley of The Kings

There are others watching us as we explore the sites of Upper Egypt.

This afternoon we crossed the Nile to visit The Valley of the Kings and Queen Hatshepsut's Temple. Virgil Powell was keen to visit the tomb of the boy king Tutankhamun.

He told us: "Tutankhamun and the entire Amarna family strikes me as alien, beginning of course with Akhenaten and Nefertiti. Look at their distended heads and tell me you don't think they look like visitors…"

My eyes were on other visitors, the international visitors milling around in the Valley today. While numbers are down on past years,

there are still a surprising number visiting the tombs.

We left Powell at the entrance. Famous as it is, the small, cramped tomb of Tutankhamun is something of a let down and so we chose a deeper tomb.

Like a near-death experience…

I murmured to Constance as we went down a descending corridor. "Don't think of going inside a tomb. Imagine instead that you're a disembodied soul moving through the tunnel of death. Rather like the classic NDE."

"NDE?" said Saneya, listening in as we went deeper into the tomb.

In spite of the heat of the day, the Egyptian had a hot jumper tied around her waist.

"Near death experience. As your soul rushes out of your body you journey through a glowing tube – like this stretching corridor with its brightly painted walls. How far do you journey? Some of these royal tombs go on for a hundred metres or more. Just like the scenes on these walls, you are surrounded on your journey by ministering beings. Who are they? Lost loved ones? The gods? Angels? There is a radiance, and around the light, radiant, welcoming beings… Then, in both the NDE and the Egyptian tomb, there comes a judgment scene where you reflect on your life and account for your actions. I am fascinated by the theory that the actual experience of death may have inspired the layout of these tombs and in fact the whole Egyptian religion."

"I'm not sure I'm going to see ministering beings welcoming me," Constance said in a fatalistic tone, "and not just because I'm blind."

An odd thing to say. Guilt about her life, perhaps? Or about the secrets that she holds?

Surrounded on your journey by ministering beings

Our secret watchers struck later when we visited the Temple of Hatshepsut at Deir el Bahari.

We climbed the long ramp of the temple.

"Sad to think this place was once the scene of a terrorist strike when gunmen came down from those cliffs and shot up sixty two tourists and Egyptians," I said.

"The Luxor massacre was a long time ago and there are now guards on the cliffs and all over the place," Saneya told us.

I saw one of two around, Kalashnikovs slung on their shoulders, dozing in the sun.

"I really miss not seeing this temple," Constance said.

"Tell me about it, Anson."

"What can I say, without throwing in the words sublime, elegant and majestic? Okay, why fight it? I see elegant terraces... sublime tiers of proto-doric columns... architecture that emerges like the dazzle of a royal appearance... and a ring of cliffs announcing its presence like a majestic fanfare of trumpets."

Today the temple was the scene of another attack.

It was not a gun battle and there were no bloodstains left on the temple stones, but it was disturbing all the same.

It began when an Egyptian man from my past stepped out from the shadows of a column, as we were about to go down the ramp and return to the vehicle.

The scene of another attack

"Would you mind lingering a moment, Mr Hunter. I need a word with you, and I have a message. You can catch up with your friends in moment."

He was the hard man who once served the former Egyptian Minister of

Culture, Saleh Haroun, the politician who was had responsibility for Egypt's Supreme Council of Antiquities.

The revolution had changed all that, but not his boss's interest in me, apparently. He looked the same, just a bit older. Tight, curly hair and a widow's peak and a whiff of tobacco smoke on his jacket. His name was Ahmed Ragab.

"Everything okay?" Virgil Powel said, giving the man a stare.

"You go ahead."

"We'll see you back at the mini bus," Constance said, overhearing the exchange.

"Thank you," my interceptor said.

"When the others were out of earshot, I said: "I thought you and your boss were out of a job now. But old habits die hard, it seems."

"You are always an interesting man to us, and so is your new client, Dr Constance Somers."

"Why is that?"

What did they know about her? Did these people still have links with the new Egyptian government, friends from the old guard in Egyptian security?

I am wondering if someone has let something slip about Constance's work and the reason for her return to Egypt. The Egyptian girl, perhaps?

It can happen so easily. An intercepted email, an overheard phone call.

An Egyptian man from my past stepped out from the shadows

"Her work is attracting unusual activity. Very special work, is it not, employing satellites up there above us, just as the gods of Egypt once looked down on the land? This is a very interesting age we live in and these are very interesting times. Difficult times to control and manage, of course. It is hard enough keeping an eye on people who sniff around Egypt's secrets on the ground. Now they explore Egypt's treasures from the sky, hundreds of kilometres above."

Ragab wasn't usually this conversational and I was wondered why.

"What is your message?"

"I am getting to that. It is curious that an academic of such standing as Doctor Somers should hire you… this famous blind archaeologist."

"I have good eyes."

"And unorthodox skills…"

Okay, at this point I become suspicious that he is dragging things out.

He's deliberately keeping me occupied. Why?

Constance.

I looked around for her, concerned, even though I knew that she had Virgil Power and the Egyptian girl to look after her.

I checked the ramp. Where was she?

Then I saw Powell. One of the tourist police down below was checking his shoulder pack, a small bag he'd brought along to tote a water bottle, sunscreen and a few personal items.

Where were the girls?

They had been separated from the men.

"Trouble always seems to follow you, Mr Hunter…"

Yes, and often in the form of this man, Ragab.

I turned to leave and he grabbed me by both arms.

"Why the hurry?"

The arms under that jacket were powerful and his grip tightened like steel bands.

The large face with the widow's peak smiled at me, perspiring in the sun.

They were after Constance.

The smile vanished when I head butted the face, smashing his nose and he reeled back against a column.

I turned and broke into a run. I sped down the ramp. A group of Japanese gave a yell of surprise and scattered like pigeons to let me through. My footsteps pounded on the stone like my pulse in my ears. An armed guard on one side of the ramp gave me an incurious gaze.

Crazy Western jogger?

The car park. They would have gone back to sit in the air-conditioned comfort of the bus.

If they got there.

I passed Virgil Powell who was rumbling in discontent at the over-zealous temple guard going through his things.

"What's wrong?"

"Constance…"

I saw our driver in front of our minibus, remonstrating with a man.

Then I saw another Egyptian man leading Constance by the arm in the other direction, with the young Egyptian girl trying to fend him off.

"Okay, stop right there!"

The man was going to bundle her into a van that stood waiting with its engine running. Saneya tugged at the man. He swung an elbow and knocked her to the ground. She gave a wailing cry. The sliding door was open and they were shoving Constance inside. I would be seconds too late. The door would slam shut and the van would go.

Not without a driver.

I got to the driver's door first and yanked it open, with one hand reached inside and grabbed the driver by his shirtsleeve and hauled him clear out of the van. Constance threw a well-aimed elbow at her attacker's face and stunned him, pulling back from the van. In another bound I was at her side. I ripped her free of the man's grasp. He jumped in the van as it drove off with a squeal of tyres. I ran with Constance, sweeping her across the parking lot.

I came within seconds of losing her.

The incident has given me new concerns. What are
these people after?

I recall that their leader, Saleh Haroun, a Sufi, had links
with the Sufi regime of Iran.

Is Constance in the middle of an international
conspiracy?

This evening I was working on my blog back at the
Winter Palace hotel when the trill of the telephone at the
bedside broke into my concentration.

Reception put a call through to me.

"Mr Anson Hunter?" an attractive young female voice
said.

"Yes."

"Are you all alone?"

"Sadly, yes."

"Your friend Bloem from Homeland said to tell you
'hey'."

"Hey."

"He also said you might help us. We need to talk to you,
privately.

We're in a van outside the hotel."

Another van. More NRO people? The twins had warned
me that I'd be contacted later.

"I'll be down."

A young, pert, redheaded girl met me outside and guided me to a parked silver Sprinter van.

"I'm Kelly. Glad you could slip away."

She slid open a side door and I went up a step into the interior. She came up behind me and dragged the door shut behind us with a firm clunk.

I found myself in a mobile office, where a man, seated in front of a desk and screen, swivelled round to face me. An Egyptian driver sat at the wheel.

"Thanks for coming."

She sat on one of the seats beside the desk and I did the same as the van pulled off into traffic along the Corniche. Well this was certainly a more polite way to meet than having a meaty hand clamped over my face, I thought.

The man at the desk, in his early forties had the careful eyes and neutrally polite manner of a government servant.

"Bloem speaks highly of your abilities."

"But not all that warmly of our friendship, no doubt."

"I'm Carpenter."

"What do we want to talk about this time?"

"Dr Constance Somers. As a so-called space archaeologist, she has made extensive use of satellite imagery in her space archaeology. Her satellite imagery analysis may have discovered something with disturbing implications."

"Disturbing for whom?" I said.

"For the world."

"So she's stumbled across something she shouldn't. Let me guess.

 Evidence that ancient aliens, who of course built the pyramids, are now returning to check on their handiwork?"

"Maybe we can explain the situation if we show you something. Do you know anything about space archaeology?"

"I've come across it in the past," I thought, recalling with a pang a young woman from The Anubis Intervention affair.

"Well things have moved along at an exponential rate in the field. Higher resolution technology, powerful new space cameras and infrared imagery can now pinpoint and record objects the size of a dinner plate under the sand and sophisticated new computer algorithms sift the sand for clues. Whereas the technology could once only penetrate a few feet below the surface, it's now going much deeper." He turned back to the screen and punched a keyboard to bring up an image on the screen.

"Here's a typical satellite view of the Saqqara plateau as seen from four hundred and thirty five miles above. Radio wave pulses at 1,700 a second are transmitted from a satellite and the backscatter echo is collected and processed to create the image. Obviously, strong backscatter reveals pyramids and other archaeological constructions."

The screen filled with a dun coloured area, showing the step pyramid and the shadows of underlying structures.

"Now when we add false colour imaging, we see this." He clicked a keyboard. The screen now filled with a multi-coloured Rorschach test of blotches in red, blue and green. "Here we see the spectral signatures of pyramids and tombs.

All pretty standard. However, as you might know, a lot of this new capability owes its existence to military intelligence technology. Dr Somers has used an array of satellite information, including NASA, the Japanese Earth Resources Satellite JERS-1 and the European Union's European Remote Sensing Satellite ERS-1 as well as optical satellite data from the French SPOT satellites, American Landsat, and Russia's KVR-1000. Not long ago, however, we believe she came by satellite imagery of an enhanced nature - Russian perhaps -

that, once analysed, may have yielded unusual information."

Satellite eye in the sky over Saqqara

"There's an elephant in the van," I said. "Her partner is a man called Virgil Powell, a player in the satellite field. Don't you think he could have provided her with these images, and what do you know about him?"

"Powell is a big government contractor with many powerful friends in Washington and around the world, but we're not sure if his organisation has this technology." He shrugged. "I suppose where she came by the images is of lesser concern right now. It's the information she has that interests us."

The van pulled up and the driver turned around and made a gesture with a pack of cigarettes.

"You've found us a quiet spot for us to talk, Ahmed? Okay, take a smoke outside and keep an eye out."

"What sort of information?" I said.

"We don't know exactly," the girl said. "But there's something peculiar down there in the concession area at Saqqara where her team has been working."

"Something that we can only describe as being of an unexplained and volatile nature."

"How do you know? Do you have an image?"

"No, we have been piecing much of this together from Intelligence work, but we have recorded sightings above Saqqara that appear to be related." He flicked up a new screen image that showed a dark area of sky and stars and thin, silvery white pulses emitting from below. They were not beams like those from a searchlight or even a laser, but a curiously organic, silver chords that twisted in the air. Spectral. Ghostly.

"They remind me of natural magnetic phenomena such as the

Aurora Borealis."

"Not at Egypt's latitude, and this is more concentrated. It also seems far from natural. Unnatural in fact. Quite eerie. NASA earth scientists are at a loss."

What has Constance found... or disturbed?

"Do you think it's something of military significance?"

"Let's just say it's a security concern."

"Here's another guess. Something belonging to another power, or even the US, has landed and lies buried under the sand, something the US does not want the Middle East, Iran most of all, getting hold of and reverse-engineering."

"I like your paranoia, Mr Hunter. You should be in Intelligence."

"All this has been intriguing and certainly been more enjoyable than your Philae briefing."

"Philae briefing?"

"When two agents hauled me aside into a dark chamber with a hand clamped over my mouth."

The man and young woman exchanged glances.

"Not us," the girl said.

"Perhaps you'd better explain," the agent called Carpenter said.

I told them. "They also gave me this." I dug into my pocket and pulled out the device that the twins had given me. The two occupants seemed to shrink to the corners of the van as if I were holding up a grenade with the pin pulled out. "It's only a tracking device."

The girl put a finger to her lips and the man held out his hand for the device. I handed it over, not sure whether I was relieved to be rid of it or more unsettled about it than before.

The man stood up, slid the device under the leg of the chair then sat down on it hard. The device gave a crack. Then he poured water from a bottle into a foam cup of and dropped the device inside.

"A precaution. Maybe too late if it's a listening device," the girl said.

"This complicates things," the man said.

"Then who were the two who grabbed me?"

"Possibly members of a group who have shown an interest in Dr Somer's work. Another hydra head of the New World Government conspiracy, looking to bring about a shining new age. Like some ugly tree with roots that have gnarled their way into the depths of our body politic, even into our military."

"They seemed quite convincing. But then so are you. Maybe it's time I asked for some credentials."

The man pulled out a wallet and flashed an identity that included a crest.

The US satellite surveillance agency

"There's something else. Local elements are taking an interest in Dr

Somers."

I told them about Saleh Haroun and his hard man, Ahmed Ragab, and about the incident at the Temple of Hatshepsut.

"Now we understand your reference to Iran."

"Okay. So what do you want me to do now?"

The man thought about it.

He was still considering the question when the driver opened the door and climbed back in and twisted in his chair.

Except it wasn't the driver, it was a swarthy young man with a silenced handgun, which he swung around and fired just two times. Two dull thuds popped like a couple of flat champagne bottles opening.

The man at the desk and the girl beside me kicked in their chairs and slumped.

"You have broken faith with us Mr Hunter. That's disappointing," the mild twin said. He unlocked the doors with the remote on the driver's keys and now the side door rumbled open to reveal Twin Two, who climbed into the van.

This one was the human gag, the one who had grabbed my mouth in a meaty hand and dragged me into a chamber at Philae.

While he held an unwavering gun over me, the other calmly drove off.

"What are we going to do with the two back there?" the driver said over his shoulder.

"Drop them off in an irrigation canal," the other said, without even glancing at the two slumped forms. "Then we'll torch this thing. We don't want to set the Egyptian authorities swarming around. An investigation could get in the road."

I now know how the Israelites felt being held captive in Egypt.

I've had a taste of it after spending a night shut in a cellar like a tomb under a village house outside Luxor, with nothing but an oil lamp, some Arab flat bread and a jug of questionable water.

I was also given a large jar as an ensuite.

The twins did not look in on me, just left me to contemplate my situation and the horror of what had happened to that young redhead and the man from the NRO.

Captive in Egypt

A few hours earlier I had been looking at images from space. Now I could barely see the walls lit by my lamp flame. Would I die down here? Or did they have plans for me?

I wondered if those plans involved Constance...

What is going to happen to her?

Guerilla archaeology

The next morning I was driven in the back of a curtained microbus into Luxor under the close guard of the twins, one at the wheel and the other beside me.

Outside The Winter Palace

"Here comes our transport to take us to Karnak," I heard Virgil Powell's muffled voice outside the curtained microbus they had parked outside the Winter Palace hotel.

"But where is Anson?" It was Constance's voice.

"He's an alternative Egyptologist. He probably made alternative plans.

I'm sure he'll turn up."

The side door slid open allowing first Saneya, then Constance and finally Powell inside. The women sat down and as it pulled off, the twin who was clamping a hand over my mouth, let go.

He lifted his handgun as he moved down the aisle towards the new arrivals.

That's when I noticed that Powell was still standing.

"Sorry, folks. Change of plan. But the good news is that we have found Anson. There he is, lurking at the back of the bus. It seems that our friend has been leaking badly to authorities and we just can't have others involved in this and so we are going to have to move things forward."

"What is happening, Virgil?" Constance said.

"Your partner has just broken off the partnership," I said from the back. "He has friends with guns. We've been hijacked."

"Virgil, answer me."

"Sorry again, Constance."

"What are you doing?"

"It's what we're all doing that you should focus your mind upon. We are now pushing on by road to Saqqara and I'm afraid we are going to have to break into your discovery site before the season's official opening next week."

"I don't understand."

"You do. You may not see, but you understand. You have found something remarkable and we want what you have found. Consider us your exploration team. Meet Kane and Kurt. Handsome, but terrible twins to cross. The twins will be our designated drivers today. It's going to be a long drive of six or seven hours, with a few breaks at safe houses and so on, and we will reach the site after dark. So sit back, relax and enjoy the ride..."

Although our journey north was not on the River Nile, but in parallel with it, I felt a current of events out of my control sweeping me up and carrying me along with it – as well as the two women who had started out on this guided tour with me, Constance and Saneya.
They didn't deserve this.
But then neither did the NRO agents deserve what had happened to them.
What was the overwhelming lure of Constance's discovery that inspired such ruthless determination?

Would we meet the same fate if things suddenly turned bad or once we had outlived our usefulness?

Our abductors kept us apart on the tourist bus, isolating us from each other in different seats, perhaps in order to prevent us from conspiring, yet what could one man, a blind woman and a young Egyptian student do against three abductors, two of whom, at least, carried firearms?

Even if I did manage to surprise the men for a moment and attempt an escape, how far could I hope to get with Constance and her assistant?

It was hopeless, but that didn't mean I couldn't play a few road games to pass the time.

"Are you all going to be boring?" I said. "How about a song for the road? Anybody?"

"It's going to be a bit of a long journey for singing," Powell said.

"Then how about a guessing game? We'll begin with you, Constance.

Give us a clue about what you found in Saqqara. Just a name, or even the first letter will do…"

"I…" Constance said.

"I? As in you, me and I?"

"I."

"Oh, not the pronoun. Hm. I… I… I? Male or female…?
Isis! There is a text that speaks of the burial place of Isis
in Lower Egypt."

"Male."

"Omigod, don't tell me. Or do tell me. It's not Imhotep?
You've found the tomb of Imhotep?"

The bus went silent.

Even the sound of the engine grew thin and far away.

Most revealing of all, Constance remained silent.

No denial. No confirmation, true, but *no denial.*

I had heard enough to send my mind into an orbit like
one of Constance's satellites.

Now a whole lot of clues clicked into place.

Powell's deep reverence for Imhotep and his remarks
about Imhotep's origins.

Then I recalled Constance's theory about Imhotep's
giving Egypt medicine purely to keep his work force
going.

Maybe there is something in that.

Imhotep as the founder of medicine is considered to be
the author of the Edwin Smith medical papyrus, a
practical treatise devoid of magical spells. The 48 cases
cited are all about injuries that would be totally
consistent with those of a labour force working on
pyramid construction. It lists examples of 27 head

injuries, 6 throat and neck injuries, 2 injuries to the clavicle, 3 injuries to the arm, 8 injuries to the sternum and ribs, 1 tumour and 1 abscess of the breast and 1 injury to the spine.

Egyptologist's are certain that Imhotep's tomb lies somewhere in the Saqqara area, probably in sight of the step pyramid he created for Djoser and Egyptologists such as Firth and Walter Emery spent much of their lives trying to track it down, without success.

Now a blind archaeologist had found it, or at least one who was now blind.

How long ago had she found it? How long had she been sitting on the secret of such a great find?

Wikipedia

The discovery of Imhotep's tomb, or even a lost cenotaph or sanctuary, would be a colossal event in Egyptology, yet it still did not explain the swirling conspiracy that surrounded the site.

Why did it interest America's satellite Intelligence office?

And why Virgil Powell?

What did they expect to find down there?

The current of events had become a spate.

Has the dust of archaeology combusted in a flash of science fiction?

Step pyramid, Saqqara, designed by Imhotep

What in hell did my eyes see when Constance finally revealed her secret in Saqqara?

Evidence of ancient visitors?

If this is the truth about ancient Egypt, the great and shining civilization that I've spent my life studying, then I am going to be the most forlorn convert in history.

I flinched as I shone my flashlight beam in the darkness. We were in an underground passage beneath the sands of Saqqara at an unknown sanctuary beyond the step pyramid.

Ahead I saw an alien, pyramid-shaped entrance bordered by swarms of eyes, dozens, hundreds... thousands.

This is just wrong for ancient Egypt.

It's as if the dust of archaeology and aeons of ancient history have suddenly combusted in a flash of science fiction.

"Tell me what you see," the blind female Egyptologist beside me said.

I searched for the right words.

Virgil Powell, the UFOlogist, spoke before I could form an answer.

"What he sees are countless alien eyes bordering a triangular doorway. He also sees the evidence that he dreads staring back at him, and his silence says that this discovery does violence to everything he knows and believes."

Ancient aliens? Just the mention of that is a career killer for anyone in Egyptology, even a renegade outsider like me, and it's probably a religion killer, too. Especially my religion, such as it is. I can recall wrestling with my faith just about every day of my working life in my chosen occupation as I go about rubbing shoulders with pagan deities and immersing myself in the religious practices of the ancient past. I haven't made it easy for myself to cling to the few, old-fashioned ideas about Christianity that I value and this sort of collision doesn't help.

It's a wrecking ball.

"Perhaps the eyes are symbolic," the blind Egyptologist said, reaching out to brush one of the raised eyes lightly with the tips of her fingers

This action of hers holds a peculiar poignancy for me as I remember it now - a blind woman wistfully touching eyes. "It could be numerical code, just as the Horus eye and its elements are now recognised as expressions of fractions."

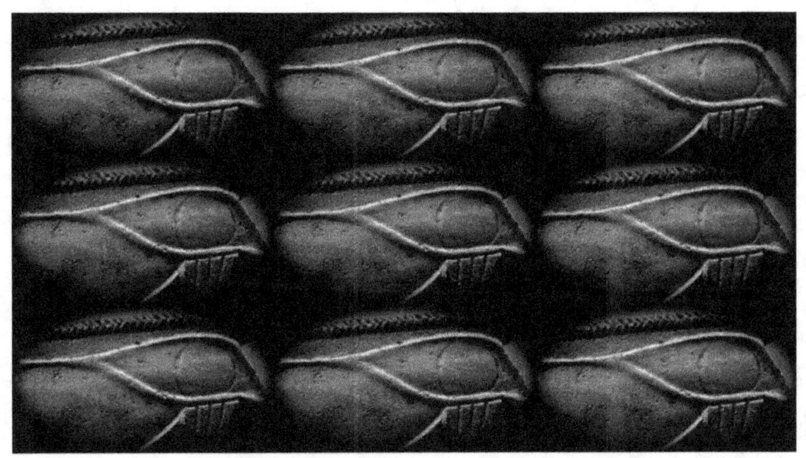

Eyes bordering a triangular doorway

I'm familiar with the ancient Egyptian fractions system based on the hieroglyph of the Horus eye. But the eyes surrounding that doorway don't look like fractions. They just look disturbing.

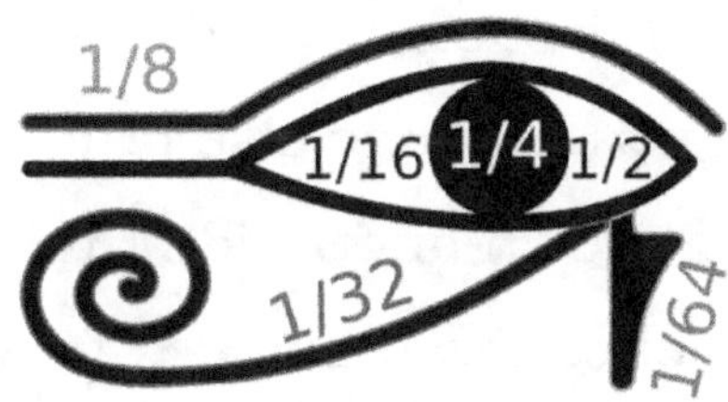

Wikipedia

Yes, the eyes have echoes of ancient Egyptian design, and carved in the wall is the illustrious name 'Imhotep', added by a later visitor in hieroglyphs that I can recognise. But the triangular doorway and the massing of stylised eyes that borders it is another matter. If this is ancient Egyptian design, then it comes from some unknown, primordial stage or else some unknown point of evolution.

Either that or it's the product of a mind warped by psychedelic drugs.

"I'm not about to leap to conclusions," I said, "especially not to outer space and to alien visitors."

"Then Constance is not the only blind one down here," the UFOlogist said. "Is it heresy to accept the truth, even for an alternative Egyptologist known for his controversial theories?"

I looked at Constance Somers. She had taken off her glasses down here and did not look like a woman who was legally blind. Her eyes shone.

"I know you are shocked by this discovery, Anson. I was stunned too when I first came across it. But now you see why I needed you. Anyone else but you would go into scholarly shut down and I didn't have time for that. I wanted to experience the radiance of a great mystery before it's too late, but I needed you to guide us on this journey, to help me find the light. This will take your special knowledge and problem-solving skills to negotiate the dangers that lie ahead and to penetrate the sanctuary. I'm sorry... I know this is not the way I hoped we'd explore this structure together. But please help me by telling me what you see."

An unsettling question arose in my mind.

What kind of tomb would a luminous intelligence such as Imhotep - an alien in his genius - engineer for himself?

Think about that. Then consider the rogue idea that Imhotep may not have been of this world...

I start to imagine creatures from movies like Alien and Prometheus, but this was not a movie. It was rock-solid-real, like the walls of the passage and the carved stone doorway in front of us.

A bizarre triangular shape

I stood with the group in front of the bizarre, triangular shaped entrance to a new tomb or sanctuary, on a threshold between scientific certainties and a new frontier of belief.

I could not have been more stunned if I had walked into a wall and was seeing stars before my eyes. First of all there was the giddy euphoria of coming across the illustrious name 'Imhotep' and the flight of imagining that came with that discovery. Was this the lost tomb that Egyptologists had spent their lives trying to find? A cenotaph? A sanctuary? Who had put the name there? The label had all the hallmarks of a visit by the tomb intruder Khaemwaset, son of Rameses II, the same historical figure that both Constance and I had been tracking.

Khaemwaset, I now see, is the converging point of our two lives.

If Khaemwaset had penetrated this underground structure ahead of us, what was he after and what had he found? Forbidden secrets? Some ancient loci of power?

Lit by our flashlights, the underground doorway lay open for entry, yet the myriad inlaid eyes surrounding the doorway seemed to project an invisible barrier.

"All those eyes seem to be watching us," the mild twin said. "They look kind of like spider's eyes..."

"...or camera lenses," the other finished

"They represent the Watchers," Virgil Powell said.

"They're cool," the geek-girl Egyptian student said, coming out of her shell. "And weird!"

"You've entered here before?" I said to the Egyptologist.

"Yes, on my own, without Saneya at the time. My sight was already failing, and I decided to come back again later with those who could help me."

She had come back here with more than help. She had come back with a pair of young killers and their leader, Powell, a mysterious UFOlogist who owned a US satellite technology company, and had links with America's military-industrial complex.

She moved ahead, her long white cane flashing ahead in our beams. The blind leading the blind and the wilfully blind, I thought as the group of people moved after her through the entranceway, she tapping the stone floor with her cane, like the exploring feeler of an insect, the rest of us flashing lights around like wary eyes.

Imhotep?

The entrance was pristine, undisturbed. How was it possible? How had Imhotep's sanctuary survived where so many others had been pillaged? Imhotep, the first great architect, inventor of the pyramid and buildings in stone, father of medicine and patron of ancient Egyptian writing, had journeyed across time through all the dangers and tumult of history to arrive thousands of years later to the reign of Rameses, Usermaatre-setepenre when the king's son Prince Khaemwaset first found it, and now it was the turn of Dr Constance Somers and this group.

Our abductors had broken through a locked gate at the dig site and she had led us here along a hidden passage. Did the survival of this sanctuary signify that Imhotep had protected it with unique defences?

Masterly worked stone and faience tiles all around, I thought, noting the peculiar symmetry of the arrangement on the walls as we moved through. But what did it all mean? This was symbolism and iconography foreign to my mind. What was its owner trying to signify? That this was the opening to an otherworldly realm where men, even explorer princes, should be wise not to enter?

Yet there were still no visible barriers to progress.

At least not yet.

What dangers could we expect? This structure must be five thousand years old.

But it wasn't any structure. It was a structure engineered by a genius. Or as Powell would have it, an alien intelligence.

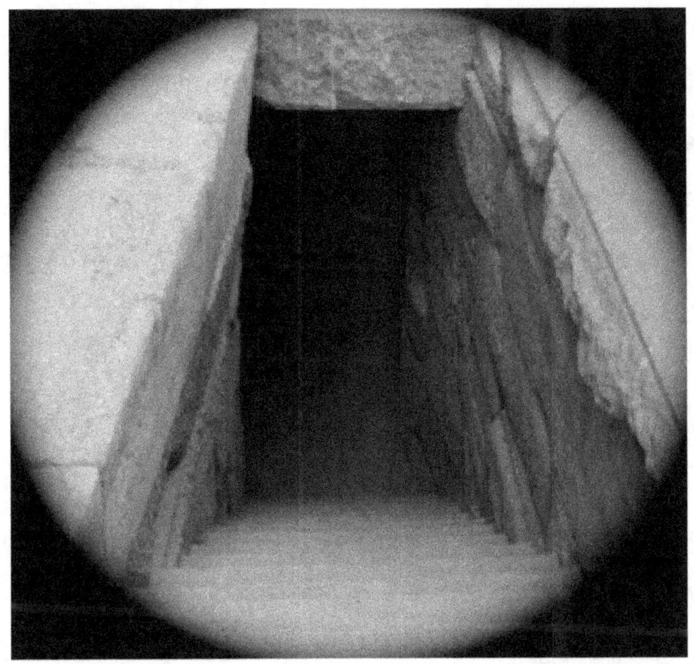

Was this a sanctuary with unique defences?

Maybe we would be wise to start viewing it that way, I thought. We should prepare ourselves for defences and tomb traps that were foreign to our experience, just as the first great monument in carved stone, the step pyramid of Djoser, conceived and built by Imhotep, was an alien concept to the world.

We went down steps and at the bottom the stone floor began dropping under our feet as we descended a ramp. The air here felt alive and charged with positive ions, instead of lying heavily on your lungs as it did in tombs and pyramids. Perhaps it was our expectations and the knowledge that we were entering a realm of the unknown that made the atmosphere crackle.

"How far does this go down?" I asked her.

"Not far," she said. "We'll come to a hall with an image of Imhotep at the entrance and guess what's on the wall beside him? A set of surgical instruments."

Now I remembered her strange behaviour at the temple of Kom Ombo where she ran her hands, curiously unsteady over carvings of forceps, scalpels, probes, sponge, saw blades, scales, scissors, hooks and more…

"Was Imhotep really such a benevolent figure to humanity? Did Imhotep have a dark agenda? I'll tell you. He gave Egypt medicine and surgery in order to keep his vast workforce going."

"Is there something you didn't like about the instruments, Constance?"

"There's something I didn't like about the hall."

An image of the deified Imhotep sprang into our flashlight beams at the end of the ramp, his elongated skull in a cap like the god Ptah. In one hand he held his staff and beside him on a wall appeared a set of surgical instruments like the one we had seen at Kom Ombo temple, yet strikingly futuristic in style.

Why did I think that this display of the tools of surgery was not here to heal, but to harm? Imhotep's small figure on the wall reminded me of a demon gatekeeper of the underworld.

"I think we've reached a Hall of Hindering," I said.

"Hindering? What do you mean, hindering?" the mild twin began.

"What are you telling us..."

"...that some obstacle's going to slow us down?"

"Or kill us. At the very least, it will punish us if we don't tread carefully. Surgical tools bear strong resemblance to instruments of torture, you may have noticed."

"This place is mind-bending," Saneya said.

I flashed my light over the doorway.

"You came this way, Constance?"

"Not this far, but somebody else did. Somebody who secretly followed me down here. I heard them behind me and I was able to hide in a recess as they passed me by and went inside. I waited outside. After a time, I heard a man's terrible cry of fear and pain. He never came out."

And now the black rectangle of the doorway leaked a dark fear into the midst of our group. What was inside there? My beam paused on the skull-capped head of Imhotep. A pitiless face. Faces like his were at work in the inquisition, bending over racks and thumbscrews as they listened to their victims' screams, evil angels certain that they were doing god's work, seraphically calm and distant from the human suffering they inflicted.

It was the face of the architect of Egypt's first pyramid. I have always believed that the most casual glance at the pyramids tells you that these were as much diabolical and soul-destroying constructions as they were monuments to ancient Egypt's belief in the survival of the soul.

And now we were entering their creator's underground hypogeum.

Powell said. "In most cases of alien abductions, abductees report being subjected to probes, operations and medical experiments."

"Then we have two possibilities," I said. "Torturers of an ancient

Egyptian kind or extra-terrestrial ones. Anyone have a preference?"

I focused my beam on individual instruments. Forceps, scalpels, probes, saw blades, scales, scissors, a sponge, hooks, cupping vessels, a dilator, a catheter, rows of flasks and prescriptions...then I went back to Imhotep. In one hand the genius held his staff, in the other a handful of plants, a blue lotus, mandrake, others I could not identify. Powerful drugs and not just medicinal. Psychedelic compounds.

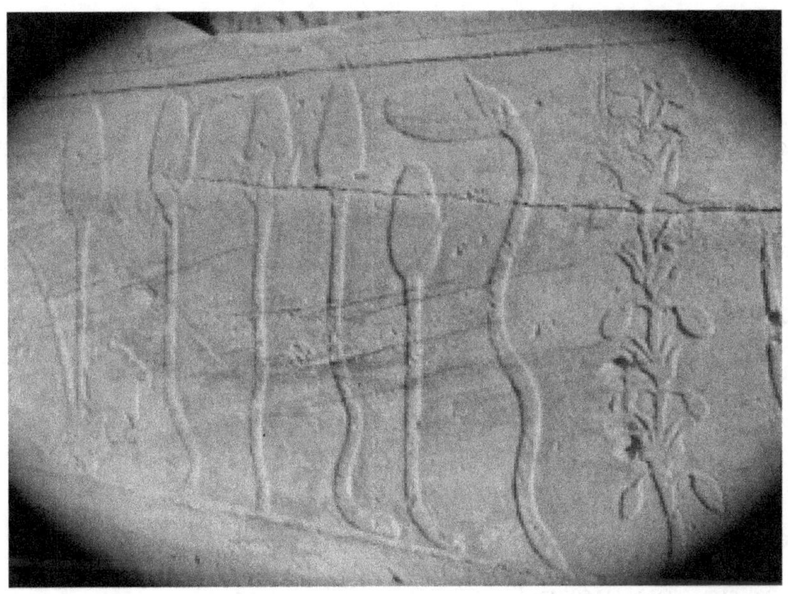

Gods are often shown holding psycho-active plants

"You go in first," Powell said to me and the hard twin gave me a nudge from behind.

I stepped into the unknown, my beam probing near-sightedly in the thick blackness. It was a hall with severe square columns. I checked the floor for traps and pits. Just a coating of powdery dust clouded the smoothly dressed stone. Strange, the dust in here. The ramp had been relatively clean. Maybe the desert sand had seeped in somehow.

"Seems okay," I said. I heard shuffles of footsteps as the others came in after me, and the tap tap of Constance's cane.

"Describe it, Anson."

Our flashlight beams flitted around the darkness.

"Columned hall, severe in the Old Kingdom style. Quite a bit of dust," I said as we moved through it. "Unusually dusty, in fact." With my flashlight held out ahead, I felt a rain of fine dust landing on my arm.

I stopped. We were all inside.

"Why have you stopped?" a twin said.

"Do you feel that in the air, settling on your skin?"

"Dust."

"I hope so."

"What do you mean?"

I felt the hall give a turn and a warmth began to steal over me and spread through my limbs. Was it the glow of the ancient divine?

Or something else?

"Move on," the twin said.

"Did anyone see that?" Powell said.

"What?"

"A beam, like a laser flash."

"No. But I feel as if I'm walking in soft fur," Constance said.

"There – again! A probe."

I hadn't seen it, but now my insides were warmly glowing and a languor stole over my body.

"This place is far out," Saneya said, then giggled.

Powell gave a grunt of surprise.

"See that?"

"What?" said the twins.

"A grey! Near that column."

"A grey? What is a grey?" Saneya said, squinting into his cone of light.

"They are the most commonly seen of the visitors..."

"Aliens... stunted little guys with big heads," Twin Two finished his sentence.

"Like Imhotep? He was a small guy with a big head." Saneya again.

"Let's move on." I flashed my beam up at the ceiling. Was something sifting down on us, something as fine as flour? Particles in the air shredded my beam.

I turned the light around, stopped. What were those things on the far wall beyond the columns? I trained my beam. Surgical instruments? Yes, but not carved into the stone, real objects, protruding. Large, cruel hooks, saw blades... bronze bladed scalpels... the walls were bristling with sharp metal.

I flashed my beam around to the opposite wall and gave a start. A body hung impaled on hooks in the wall... was this the man who had gone in ahead of Constance, the one who had cried out in terrible fear and pain?

Now the sight vanished from view as I passed a column.

"Over there," I said.

"What did you see?" Constance said.

"An alien?"

"A man. Or what's left of him. Someone who came this way before and never got out. Your stalker."

A nightmare of visions

"More greys. I'm telling you, people, they are everywhere. Massing. Like those eyes at the entrance," Powell said.

"Stay together," I said, "and whatever you do, keep away from the walls."

Now I saw the floor sway and melt. A pit fell open up on the side of us.

What was happening?

What was Imhotep doing to us? I had a memory flash of the demigod standing at the doorway, staff in one hand

and plants in the other. Maybe it was not Imhotep doing this to us, but the objects in his hands.

Egypt's gods were often shown holding plants with psychoactive properties – powerful, reality-altering drugs.

The powder drifting from the ceiling.

Were we all caught up in the grip of hallucinogens?

"They're gathering to block our way," Powell said. "We're going to have to go around them."

"Stay in the middle or you'll end down a pit, or worse, hanging from a hook. Constance?"

"Yes."

"You go ahead. You lead us. Everybody else, close your eyes. Do it! Get into line and touch the shoulder of the one in front – or you're going to die."

"Follow the blind girl?"

"Do it – or die."

"Is this a party game?" Saneya said.

I took hold of Constance's shoulder and felt a hand clamp on mine. I screwed my eyes tightly shut.

"Keep going, Constance."

"Here we go."

Tap, tap, tap.

"We are the six blind mice," Saneya said.

"Did someone say, mice?" Constance said.

"Don't listen to her. Just keep going."

The blind snake-line of people threaded its way between the columns.

But even in the greater darkness of my thoughts, there was no escape.

I saw bodies hanging from hooks and now impish beings in skullcaps cutting and sawing at them with surgeon's tools. Limbs dropped to the stone floor. A hanging body writhed as a hook was rammed up its nostrils, then twisted around to emerge with gobbets of quivering brain. Hearts, lungs and livers, fell with the slaps of wet fish on the stone and blood rained down on the floor.

A nightmare of visions

Tap, tap, tap.

A blind woman is our hope. The blind leading the blind through a nightmare of visions.

"Stop!"

The tapping ceased and the line of people telescoped behind the blind archaeologist.

"What do you see? I mean feel."

"Nothing. The floor drops away. A pit."

A real pit? Or had some hallucinogenic vision entered her darkness?

"Are you sure?"

She rapped her cane on a stone edge.

"Here's where it begins. It feels deep. I can feel it drawing me in."

Tap, tap. Tap, tap, tap. We heard her long white cane exploring the edge.

"You're getting up a rhythm there," mild twin said.

"It's an Egyptian line dance."

"We'll edge around it – carefully."

She moved and the blindworm of people followed. I recalled the day I met this young blind woman who was now leading us through darkness and asked myself the question: *Is a blind woman planning to lead me along some unknown path? Towards what?*

How close were we to the edge of a pit? I allowed myself a peep. Error. A vision of a sharp bronze hook like a scythe flashed from the darkness below. I ducked and hauled Constance aside.

"No, Anson! There's a pit on the other side too!"

I'd let in the nightmare and was giving it power to destroy me. I closed my eyes again. Just focus on that calming tap, tap, tap. Like a heartbeat, a ticking watch… a time bomb.

What lay ahead? Another pit? A doorway at the end that would take us out of this hall?

Languor stole over me like a soft, warm blanket. Powerful compounds in my bloodstream spread inertia to all my limbs.

Although my eyes were tightly shut, I could detect the glow of our flashlight through my eyelids and ghostly images floated in the semi-darkness like the light scars left after looking at bright lights. The shapes shifted, morphed into figures. Malignant imps like Imhotep, emerged from behind columns to watch us, like the myriad eyes at the entrance…

Did drugs explain their presence?

What if all alien visitations are actually the products of the hallucinogenic influences of the modern world? Maybe there are no alien visitors, just psychonauts crossing the galaxies of our collective imagination, their ships powered by hallucinogens.

We see what life conditions us to see.

I see demons, Powell sees aliens.

Which one of these was Imhotep? Demon or alien, or one and the same thing, a fallen being from the sky? Was Imhotep's determination to build the first monument in stone a demonic urge?

Then I had a vision. I saw a being in a skull-cap sitting under a shaded chair in a desert plain and a pyramid of human bodies stacked high where stone blocks should be, rising in six tiers to the sky.

There were precisely one and a half million souls in the Old Kingdom at that time. And one and a half million blocks of stone in the step pyramid.

Imhotep was constructing a pyramid of damned souls. Why didn't I see that before? Psychoactive drugs could bring on higher states of consciousness and new perceptions. Did it take this shamanic vision to reveal the truth?

At the beginning of pharaoh Djoser's reign the kingdom was still recovering from a terrible civil war between the north and the south. Imhotep took this opportunity to forge a nation-building unity in the shape of the world's first pyramid. *The salvation of the king was the paramount purpose and the people worked with a will because it was a collective salvation.* If the king survived, then so would the nation and all who existed in Egypt. And so they pledged their souls to Imhotep's grand design and all bent beneath his rod.

I pictured the rod in the demigod's hand, thin and shining like a crack between dimensions.

The demons and aliens did not want human bodies for their experimentation.

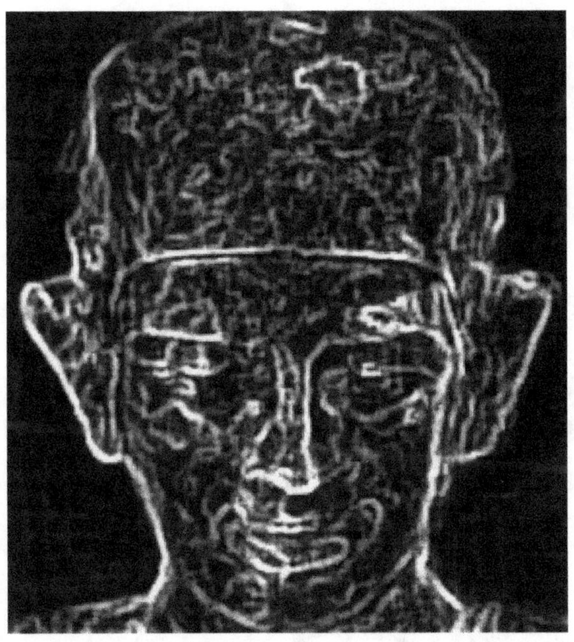

Imhotep was constructing a pyramid of damned souls

They wanted to claim human souls.

Imhotep, the genius who 'fell from the sky', began the demonic,

Luciferian work of stealing souls and the pyramid was his diabolical machine.

And so pharaoh enslaved Egyptians, and not just the Israelites, and he enslaved them for eternity. And the horror continued, reaching its height in the construction of the Great Pyramid.

The Great Pyramid had two point three million stone blocks, exactly the same number as the population of Old Kingdom in Khufu's dynasty.

But if Imhotep was creating monuments of bound souls, where did these souls go? Were they streamed into an alien world amid the circumpolar stars, just as pharaoh's soul was said to journey through open shafts in the pyramid carefully aligned with the heavens?

I recalled the words of the NRO man. *"We have recorded sightings above Saqqara that appear to be related." He flicked up a new screen image that showed a dark area of sky and stars and thin, silvery white pulses emitting from below. They were not beams like those from a searchlight or even a laser, but a curiously organic, silver chords that twisted in the air. Spectral. Ghostly.*

The energy of souls?

Did they populate an underworld of the damned? Or did the souls go to form the Land of the Dead, creating ancient Egypt's funerary mythology?

Perhaps the blind archaeologist was leading us to damnation…

Where did we turn in this darkness? I found myself turning for help to a shaky faith and I uttered a jumbled prayer.

"I've found the doorway," Constance said. "We can go through."

"Constance, what is this place?" I said. "Have we entered a loci of unspeakable evil?"

"No, unspeakable power and I am drawing closer to it. We followed our blind guide out of the hall and opened our eyes to find our flashlights illuminating a long gallery.

"Some trip."

"Maybe you'll all believe me now," Powell said. "There were palpable, otherworldly forces in there."

"Yes, but which other world?" I said. "The underworld?"

We arrived at another doorway.

Underworld demons

A second Hall of Hindering?

This time an image of Imhotep showed him in the company of the god of magic, Heka, a bearded deity who held crossed serpents in his hands.

"We have met Imhotep the Master Physician and now we meet Imhotep the Master of Magic and sacred words of power. This is

Imhotep, the wizard."

"You still think this is all about magic and the good versus evil polarity, without considering a third option, the non-human, extra-terrestrial evidence?" Virgil Powell said.

I ignored him and turned my mind to what might face us in the next hall. Another mind-altering attack? Or pure evil?

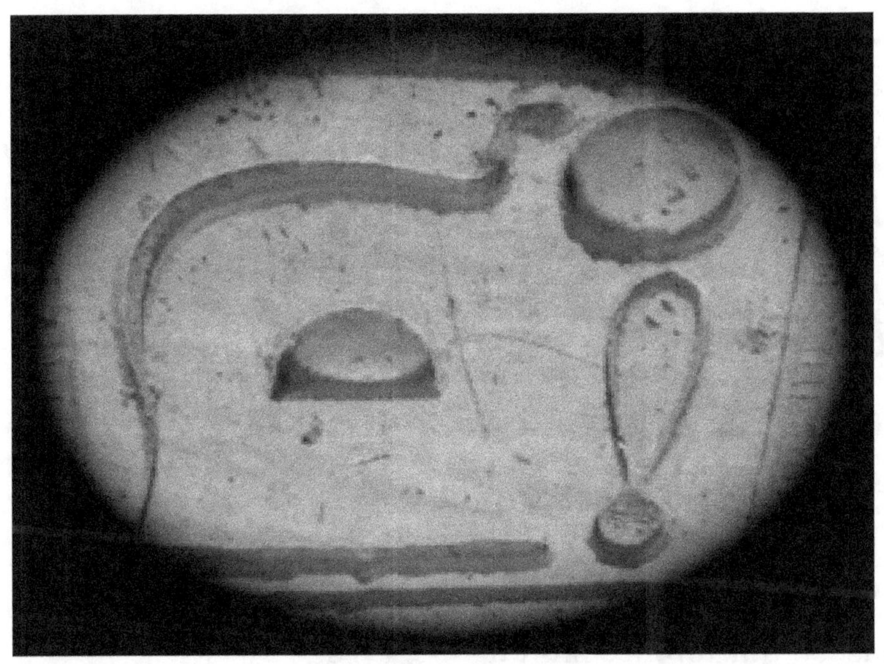

"A snake here?"

"What do you see, Anson?"

"Imhotep again, staff in hand and behind him, Heka, carrying two crossed snakes in front of his body."

"The Egyptian god of magic and spells. Do you want me to go in first?"

"No. I'm supposed to be the guide. I hope I can do as well as you did."

I moved in through the doorway ahead of the others.

The previous Hall of Hindering had directed a subtle attack that lay siege to our minds and senses with the intent of driving us to physical destruction in pits and cruel hooks and blades. What kind of an attack could we expect from Heka, god of Egyptian magic?

An inspection in my flashlight beam revealed no dust on the stone floor here.

Yet we must still be in the grip of the psycho-active powder, I guessed, for no sooner had we all gathered, our lights probing nervously around, than I gave a start as I heard a metallic-sounding scuttle among the columns.

"Keep going," the UFOlogist said.

We moved on through the hall like a long nervous insect, our torches shining like eyes.

It surged into my torch beam. I shuddered. A demon scorpion, for that was all it could have been on such a scale, spread its claws like a combative wrestler while its tail curved wickedly over its back. Most horrific of all, its scaly skin was alive and moving, seething with smaller scorpions and they now streamed off her back. Selkhet, the scorpion goddess? The mother scorpion launched an armada of smaller attackers who fanned out and formed two pincer columns like a giant scorpion's claws to converge on the advancing line of intruders. Then, in a blink, the two pincer columns of scorpions transformed themselves and solidified into the claws of yet another vast scorpion with scales like the plates of an armoured tank.

"Here it comes!"

"What?"

"Scorpion."

Couldn't they see it? I blinked and it was gone, scuttling out of view behind the columns.

"Watch out! A snake."

"A snake, here?"

"With two heads," a twin said. "No, it's two snakes - joined."

Twin snakes, conjoined. Their worst nightmare.

"I see shapes gathering around my light," Saneya said.

"Angry creatures."

"Holograms," Powell said, "designed to put us off."

"Keep going."

Curious, the pillars. They were smoother than the ones in the previous halls, rounded and tapered sharply to a point at the base and others reached up from the floor and their points fell short of the ceiling. The floor had

changed. Water must have come in here and left mould.
My foot slid from under me and I struggled to right
myself.

"I see angry creatures gathering around my light."

I shone my light down to reveal a shine of slime on the
purplish floor. I shivered as a breath came through the
columns to brush against us and behind it a hiss like a
distant breaker at the beach, but now the hiss rose and
the columns gave a judder and I knew that this was not
a hall and the columns were not stone, but fangs. We
were walking between the demonic jaws of the great
reptile Devourer of the underworld.

Apophis, the snake of chaos and outer darkness that swallowed the sun each night was about to swallow us. The mouth opened wide to slam down on the line of intruders.

We had to run.

"This is a trap! We've got to get out of here. Go back!"

"No. We must be near the end. Can you see a door ahead?" Constance said.

"Lots of doors."

Were they like the doors in the great wall that ran around the step pyramid, thirteen false doors and only one real one?

Was there time to run back? No. The teeth at the back of the jaws would meet first as the jaws slammed shut. Running forward would give us the best chance... if we could pass through a door.

Now I saw that there were in fact eight doorways, each one giving onto Stygian blackness.

"Which door?"

"Make a decision, Anson. I trust you."

The doors might all lead to traps, pits, blades, spikes, or worse.

But I had to believe that there was a mind behind this place that wanted, dared us, to progress, if we could survive the onslaught.

I heard a rumble above my head and felt a rumble beneath my feet.

The jaws were closing fast.

There was no time to weigh my decision. Eight doorways... the number eight... This was a hall of magic. All magic drew its power from the forces of original creation and the original creators were the Ogdoad, eight mysterious alien-like creature gods who swam in the slime and ooze of the primordial ocean, four males and four females. These progenitors were Amun and Amaunet demiurges of invisibility, Nun and Naunet of water, Heh and Hauhet of infinity, and Kek and

Kauket of darkness. Eight doors, four pairs.

Perhaps... I sprinted ahead to the first door and thrust my hand into the darkness. The darkness felt damp. The same with the next. These were the doorways of Nun and Naunet, representing water.

Which doorway?

"Hurry, Anson!"

I cowered from the descending roof and ran to the next two doorways. The darkness was impenetrable. The doorways of Kek and Kauket, demiurges of darkness. At the next doorway, my hand and flashlight disappeared completely. The doors of the Invisible Ones, Amun and Amaunet. The last pair of doors looked an infinity away, but I did not have to check the last pair. They must belong to Heh and Hauhet, gods of infinity.

Amun was the unseen one, god of invisibility and it was said that he was preeminent among equals and as he went like an invisible wind over the face of the waters, his breath coagulated the surface and excited the sexual

147

coupling of the four pairs of gods and goddesses to begin the act of creation.

"This one!"

I guided Constance through it and the others rushed in after her. I made a dive, the descending ceiling crashing behind me, but now it was not a serpent, but shattered stone, sending pieces like shrapnel raining against the soles of my shoes.

We lay there, waiting for the rumbling to stop.

My flashlight beam picked out their shapes as I climbed to my feet. We had all made it.

Dust pricked in my lungs.

We were now inside a corridor.

I went ahead, feeling a kind of growing density in the air as if we were approaching a force field. Our footsteps in the corridor, twisted like sound in a tube, distorting in my ears. We were drawing closer to a presence.

What was that presence? Divine?

Alien? Demonic?

I almost dreaded the collision with my beliefs and knowledge that I sensed was coming.

We stopped at the next door, which showed Imhotep in a new guise, standing beside a goddess.

"Imhotep the Master architect," I said. "In the company of the goddess Seshat, she who stretches the measuring cord for a new foundation."

I felt a tingle in the air as we moved inside.

"We're reaching the source," Powell said.

The door opened up onto a cult chapel. Our flashlight beams fell on a mound of six tiers, like a step pyramid, and at its peak, an enclosed structure that appeared to shed light from a hole in its front.

"What is it, Anson?"

"Imhotep's serdab."

"Okay, what's that?" a twin said.

"A secret, enclosed chamber that holds the *ka* statue of the dead. Charged with heka, or sacred magic, it is one and the same as the dead body of the tomb owner. You will see a hole in the wall in the front where the statue can peer out and also receive the fragrance of offerings.

"You mean a being may be inside there in some kind of state?" Virgil

Powell said. "Let's take a look."

"I'll go up," a twin said.

While the others looked on, he scaled up the steps of the underground pyramid to arrive at the top where the serdab stood, streaming light like a magic lantern from the hole in the front.

He peered inside.

"Can you see anything?" Powell said, echoing the question of Lord Carnarvon to Howard Carter as they stood at the threshold of Tutankhamun's treasures.

"An alien-looking guy holding a shining stick."

"A grey?"

"A little guy in a skull cap. Stone carving, I guess. It kind of glows like a burning candle in my light."

"Alabaster," I said.

"Yep. But that thing in his hand is alive, sparking. Some kind of white metal."

"His staff of power. Maybe electrum."

All of Egypt bowed under the rod of Imhotep.

Maybe this rod was the genesis of all wands of magic and power, yet was one of far greater malignancy. Like the power held within a fuel rod in a nuclear reactor, it held the absorbed power of countless damned souls.

Where was Imhotep himself? Somewhere beyond this chapel there might be a shaft, probably rubble-filled that would lead to his sarcophagus - if this place was in fact a tomb and not a sanctuary or cenotaph. The possibility of finding his remains did not seem to matter to this group.

"I think we've found what we have come for," Powell said. "Break open the chamber."

"You can't," I said, grabbing his arm.

"Can't we?" The young man drew the handgun from his belt and pointed it at me and I let go. Then he swung a satchel off his shoulder. "A little explosive should do it." We shrank from the pyramid and crouched low, blocking our ears, as a crack of thunder sent a rockslide of shattered blocks tumbling down one face of the pyramid.

"The rest of you stay down here."
Powell and the twins went back up the mound. They reached the top and speared the smoking interior with their flashlight beams.
"Is it damaged?" Constance called up to them in an anxious voice.
"The statue?"
"No, the staff."
"Both okay."
 "I can reach inside and take it," Powell said.
Anson saw him lean in and grasp at something and now a fulmination lit the chapel and with it came a terrible cry. Powell fell back, his body sprouting blue sparks. He tottered then tumbled down the pyramid, his body thudding on each step until he landed on the floor on his back. It was as if he had grabbed a high voltage

wire. A wisp of smoke trailed from the aghast, open tear of his mouth. The bird-like eyes were hard and hopeful, but he was clearly dead.

"What just happened?" Constance said.

"Something blasted Virgil when he touched the staff."

"Is he -?"

"Yes."

"Does he have it?"

"No."

She was more concerned about the artefact than about her ex-partner, I realized.

That was almost as shocking as the man's end.

A mound like the step pyramid

"That's too bad. But we're not going back empty handed," the twin said.

The twin took off his jacket, clearly intending to insulate himself from the lethal lightning rod.

He wrapped it around his hand and reached into the chamber.

"Got it!" He gave it a yank. Now let's take a look at it."

Lightning cracked across the chamber again and for a second it illuminated the stricken face of the young man who convulsed as sparks burst from his body, leaping from his eyes and mouth. He slumped, dropping the staff and it started to roll towards his brother. His brother jumped away and lost his footing and with a startled yell went tumbling and sliding down the opposite side.

The rod meanwhile rolled over the brink and fell, tinkling and sparking, tier after tier, to roll up to the feet of the blind archaeologist.

She bent.

"Don't."

I tried to reach her and stop her but she already had it in her hand and in my light cone she rose with it, smiling, aglow. Was she immune to its power because she could not see it?

"I have it, Anson, the light I have been searching for!"

Was that the light she wanted?

She crossed the two wands like Heka's crossed serpents.

The image flared in my light like a perverted cross of fire.

"That's not light, it's something else... damnation, evil, a deeper darkness than you already know."

"Then I am sorry for you, Anson."

She turned and went back to the doorway, carrying the staff of Imhotep and her own long white cane.

Saneya ran after her.

Before I could move, the crash of a gunshot grabbed the chamber and shook it, but the fallen twin had lost his flashlight and was aiming wildly. A wind smashed my torch from his hand and now the chapel was plunged into darkness.

Constance was gone.

I winced, nursing a stunned hand.

The darkness was drowning. We were shut in this darkness as surely as if a roof had collapsed.

I heard the faint tapping sounds fading in the distance.

Only the blind could lead me out of here.

I went after the tapping and followed the sound until I lost it.

A new and greater darkness

I had been blind to her dream and now that she was gone I was left totally blind. A new and greater darkness entered me. Without her guidance, there was no chance I could find my way out of here. She had hungered for the light and now I did.

I didn't have a prayer. Prayer?

Your word is a lamp to my feet and a light for my path.

I am the way....

I...

My mind made a bizarre leap.

iPhone...

The screen could give me light.

I dug the phone out of a pocket and switched it on to produce a dim fan of light. Not much, but the glow of the phone screen was the next best thing to a call from police rescue.

Not that there was a chance of finding phone reception down here.

I wished then that I'd downloaded one of those apps that turned the screen into a flashlight, but the glow was enough to provide some guidance as I picked my way through the rubble and the smashed columns of the Hall of Heka.

If Khaemwaset had come this way, how had he avoided setting off the collapse? Perhaps he knew a way to avoid it. And why, as a seeker of forbidden power, had he not taken the staff of Imhotep? Did he recognize its terrible meaning and decide against touching it?

What did that say about this awful talisman of power?

The twin was no less resourceful, I discovered.

I heard a sound of shifting rubble and looked back over my shoulder to see his haze of light scanning the darkness.

The murderous twin was lighting his way using the screen of his mobile phone.

If we get out of here he is not going to let me live, I thought. I've been a witness to his crimes.

I picked up my pace.

Here came the doorway to the Hall of Medicine... and the chamber of hallucinogenic attack.

Constance, where are you when I need you?

There was only one safe way through this hall of hindering and that was Constance's way – blind and by touch. It gave me an idea.

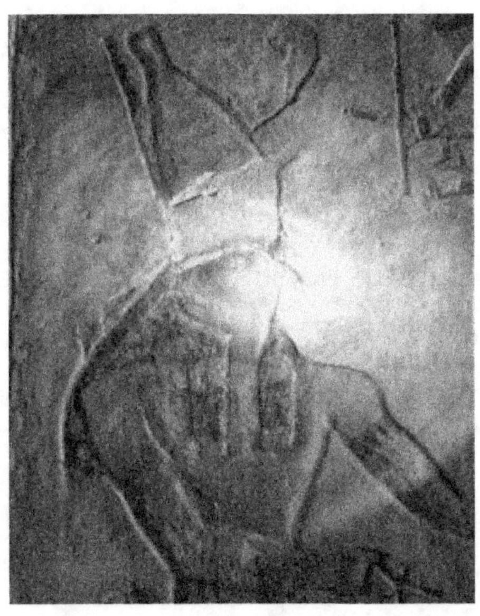

A haze of light in the darkness

I flicked off my iPhone and dropped to my knees and began a crawl across the space in darkness, feeling ahead for pits or obstacles.

Hopefully Constance was not on the young man's mind and he would stay on his feet and rely on his light and eyes.

Here came the powder rain again, landing softly like mist on my skin.

I limited my breathing, drawing shallowly through my nose. I hoped he would do the opposite.

Were there actual pits in here? Or had the mind-altering compounds opened up imaginary dangers?

I found out. My exploring hand slid suddenly and went over a rim and I fell flat on my chest. My arm dangled in a void. Some of the dangers were phantasms that came from the darkness, others were real. Don't look. I remembered the scene of the alien-like imps hacking with blades at human bodies and the sight of the dead body hanging from hooks on the wall.

I crawled around the invisible pit, reached the straight again.

Keep to the middle of the hall, between the pillars.

"Hey, Egyptologist, I know you're in here."

Company.

Great.

What now?

I was defenceless, unless I could use the psychedelic environment against him. Get him breathing heavily. Accelerate a drug-induced psychosis.

"They say twins share everything – including a brain. Sad your half-wit brother is dead."

I heard the twin draw in a breath and release it a slow, ragged sigh.

Good, take a big drag on that stuff.

"Let's work together, Mr Hunter. Turn your cell-phone on," he said reasonably. "Two lights will be better than one."

"There you go with the twin thing. Maybe it should have been you who grabbed that rod and fried on the pyramid. Did you see how your brother lit up? He was really smoking back there."

"Shut it."

"Now you're even sounding like him. You see, I think you just lost your personality back there. All you ever were was a pale reflection and now you barely exist. You should be happy to stay down here in the shadows. It's what you were born to do. Living in your brother's shadow."

The twin was coming closer. I could see a faint pink glow through my closed eyelids. Another few steps and I would be trapped in the pursuer's light beam, exposing my vulnerable position flat on the floor.

"Take a shot. You can hear my voice, can't you? Or maybe you can hear other things? Greys scuttling around with their probes. Hooks, scalpels, saw blades. It's a pity they'll only get the poor specimen to work on with you, instead of your brother, but they're circling."

The twin swore.

"They're coming?"

A spurt of light from the gun barrel ignited the darkness in the bang of a gunshot. A wind ripped over my head. Had the brief spurt of light revealed me? The next shot might be lower.

I rolled sideways and slid into emptiness.

I snapped finger-claws on an edge and my body slammed into the side of a pit. I saw another brief flash of impact as my face slammed into stone and I felt blood trickle down my lips.

I hung in an ancient Egyptian eternity.

The twin's footsteps came closer. The footsteps stopped. A glow reached into my eyelids. Has he found me hanging here?

Maybe I should just let go and find out the answers to the mystery of death and the soul that I had spent my life exploring. Was extinction waiting for me? Or something else?

I am hanging over the infernal pit, I thought. Maybe hell is where I belong, and where I was always going with my love and obsession for a pagan past. I pictured mediaeval demons with hooks and rakes below trying to drag me into the abyss.

"Get away from me!"

Screaming filled my ears and the roar of an explosion. Tormented souls below – or one tormented soul above?

I heard another roar of a gunshot then a trailing scream as a body sailed past me, going so close that it brushed my back.

The twin had tumbled into the blackness.

Lifting yourself from a hanging position is next to impossible, even for a wiry body with a good muscle to weight ratio. I raised one leg and tried to swing it over the rim. The exertion brought a cold sweat.

I felt the tremor of extremity and my brain recoiled at the approach of annihilation. The only hope was a body lift. I steeled my fingertips and knotted the muscles in my shoulders, back and arms. I heaved.

The weight of my body and the added weight of my imaginings tugged against my effort. Were there hooks in me, holding me back, drawing me down? I raised myself to my chin. Did I dare release one hand and make a grab for the surface to find a handhold? Maybe there was a crack in the stone surface to grip on to. I would get one chance. A single-handed grip would only hold for a second and then would give way and I would slip into the void.

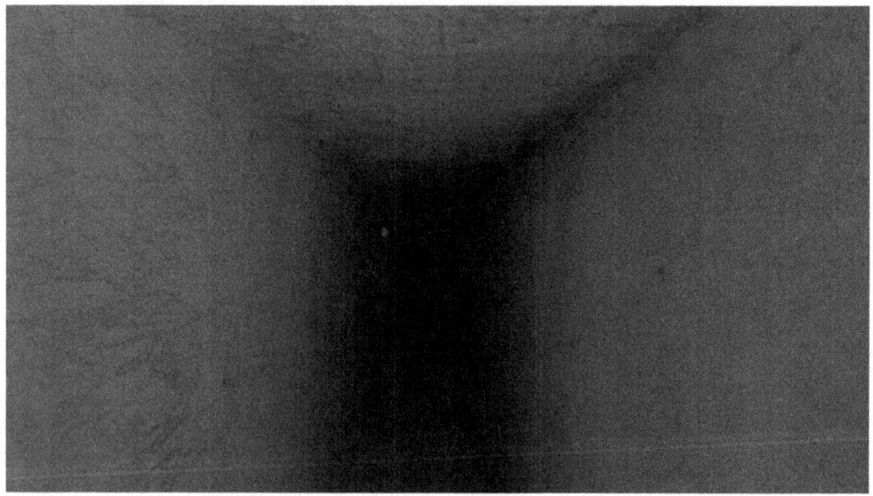

I hung in an ancient Egyptian eternity

One, two... I flung out my right hand and raked the floor for a handhold, a crack, the base of a column, anything. Nothing. My nails slid back over smooth, powdery stone. I was slipping. My sweat soaked fingers were giving. Too late I brought back the hand. Nothing could save me. A light flashed above and a grip like a manacle clamped sround my wrist.

"They thought you may need some friendly support, somebody who knows what you get up to – and they were right."

Bloem. Here? Surprise and blessed relief surged through my swinging body. I heard the big man grunt and then felt myself being hoisted back to the top.

"This time Homeland has got you out of a hole."

The dust settles

Soul-destroying constructions?

Today I am more convinced than ever that the pyramids are as much diabolical and soul-destroying constructions as they are monuments to the eternal survival of the soul. And Imhotep was their creator. With the chaos in archaeology right now - the collateral damage of

Egypt's revolution - it may be decades before this new Saqqara system is properly explored, that's if looters don't get to it first and destroy it.

Constance and Saneya slipped out of Egypt and returned to the

United States. Questioned by US authorities, Constance claims tohave lost the Imhotep artefact amid the rubble of the sanctuary and the struggle of her escape.

I was blind about her, but then I often am about women.

I was never going to have eyes only for her, and she was never going to have ears only for me. She was a scientist first and foremost, as Powell had warned me.

I hope to visit her to find out the truth for myself, but I am tied up in Egypt in lengthy police and antiquities investigations.

Constance found the light that she hungered for and nothing would have made her let go of it, I am certain...

I have a nightmare

Like an ancient Egyptian with a staff of office.

I escaped the tomb traps of Imhotep, but I have a nightmare.

I see a young blind woman in dark glasses and carrying a long cane in her hand. Perhaps she has joined a group of visitors on a tour of the US Capitol in Washington. She walks into the halls of power and her cane goes *tap, tap, tap* on the black and white marble tiles, echoing in space. It looks very much like the long cane that guided her footsteps in the past and she carries it with an air of authority like an ancient Egyptian with a staff of office. But the staff she is holding in her hand and bringing into the world's greatest seat of power will lead humankind into a frightening night.

This rod is the genesis of all wands of magic and power, yet an instrument of far greater malignancy. Like the power held within a fuel rod in a nuclear reactor, it holds the absorbed power of countless damned souls.

US Capitol. Wikipedia

THE END

About Roy Lester Pond

Roy Lester Pond is a prolific author of ancient Egypt-inspired fiction. His depth of knowledge comes from a lifetime spent studying ancient Egypt and Egyptian archaeology. He has been to Egypt on numerous research trips. Roy is fascinated by the mystery of ancient Egypt and its potency and relevance for today's world. 'The Smiting Texts' was his first archaeological thriller, followed by a series featuring renegade Egyptologist Anson Hunter, as well as other stand-alone adventures. Roy spent much of his life in Africa and now lives in Australia. Roy Tweets regularly about Egypt and adventure fiction writing under the Twittername "Egyptsnippets" and writes a blog 'Ancient Egypt

Fiction&Facts'.

Mystery of Egypt Collection by Roy Lester Pond

The Egyptian adventure series featuring Anson Hunter, alternative Egyptologist, battling dangers from the ancient past:-

ROY LESTER POND
THE SMITING TEXTS
HATHOR'S HOLOCAUST
THE IBIS APOCALYPSE
A BOATLOAD OF EGYPTOLOGISTS, A NIGHT OF DIVINE JUDGEMENT
THE NIGHT OF ANUBIS CRUISE
ROY LESTER POND
ROY LESTER POND
THE FORBIDDEN GLYPHS
EGYPT EYES
ANSON HUNTER ARCHAEOLOGY THRILLER
Roy Lester Pond
ROY LESTER POND
THE GOD DIG
ARTEFACT
ROY LESTER POND
AN ANSON HUNTER THRILLER
ALEXANDER'S LOST EGYPTIAN ORACLE
ROY LESTER POND

New

THE ANSON HUNTER series or archaeological mystery adventures

Hidden dangers from Egypt's past, modern-day conspiracies that take their impetus from Egypt's ancient mysteries.

The Smiting Texts, Hathor's Holocaust, The Ibis
Apocalypse, Hidden Egypt - The Night of Anubis, Egypt
Eyes, The Forbidden

The first three Anson Hunter novels in the 9-novel series
– in one Kindle edition. Fiction's favourite independent,
renegade Egyptologist. The Smiting Texts, Hathor's
Holocaust, The Ibis Apocalypse
*****5-star fiction Amazon/Goodreads

THE EGYPTIAN MYTHOLOGY MURDERS

A mummy named Isis is taken to a hospital for a non-invasive imaging scan… so begins a mystery and a string of deaths.

An ancient cycle unfolds in modern day London - and a search for eternal love.

Can Jennefer, a young trainee museum curator and Jon, a police antiquities unit detective, stop the killings in time before a terrible culmination of events?

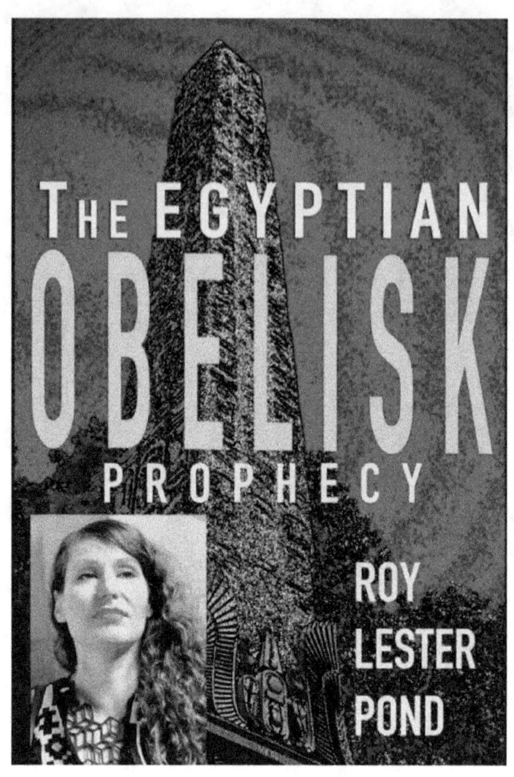

The EGYPTIAN OBELISK Prophecy

What was the Obelisk Prophecy?

The exciting fiction sequel to 'The Egyptian Mythology Murders'.

Detectives and Egyptologists are in sister professions. Now the unusual team of Jennefer, an Egyptologist museum curator, and Jon, an arts and antiquities policeman, is back together in 'The Obelisk Prophecy". Egyptian obelisks are potent symbols that pierce the skies around the world. London, New York, The Vatican…

But now one obelisk represents the clue to a world-threatening mystery.

Working against secret enemies the team must race to find and penetrate the riddle of the one obelisk on earth that holds the key to salvation.

THE EGYPTIAN CROCODILE QUEEN

When a new blockbuster ancient Egyptian exhibition arrives, mysterious events and a string of killings soon follow.

The investigative team of Jennefer, a curator, and Jon a police antiquities detective, must track down the

shocking truth in a hidden underworld beneath the city
- and discover a shocking secret from ancient Egypt,
linked to a modern day conspiracy that takes its
impetus from the ancient past.
In the unnerving footsteps of THE EGYPTIAN
MYTHOLOGY MURDERS and THE OBELISK
PROPHECY.

THE EGYPTIAN MUMMY WRAP MURDERS

4th book in the enthralling 'Egyptian Mythology
Murders' mystery series.
The spell of a vintage reel of film shot at a dig site in
Egypt in the early 1900s.
A crumbling mummy in the private museum collection
of a Grand English Castle today.

A mummy called Nephthys, the same name as the Egyptian goddess who wove the cloth mummy wrappings of Osiris, called the 'Tresses of Nephthys'.
A series of graphic murders...
Is the terrifying onslaught building to an event that will affect the world?
And what is the secret of the eerie, nonverbal young daughter of the Earl?
Investigative team of Jennefer, a British Museum Egyptologist Curator, and her partner Jon, an Antiques Unit Detective, have just hours to stop a countdown to catastrophe.

**TRILOGY. THE EGYPTIAN MYTHOLOGY MURDERS:
3 TITLES IN ONE EDITION**

Ancient Egypt resurrected...

3 Egyptian mythology-driven mystery thrillers set in the modern day, but with a twist of the ancient unknown.

A unique investigative team of Jennefer, a museum curator, and Jon a London antiquities detective - two very different people who work in 'kindred professions'...

The X-Files meets 'The Mummy'...

- THE EGYPTIAN MYTHOLOGY MURDERS

A mummy named Isis is taken to a hospital for a non-invasive imaging scan... so begins a mystery and a string of deaths.

An ancient cycle unfolds in modern day London - and a search for eternal love.

Can Jennefer, a young trainee museum curator and Jon, a police antiquities unit detective, stop the killings in time before a terrible culmination of events?

- OBELISK One Egyptian obelisk is the key to saving civilization

- THE CROCODILE QUEEN MYSYERY An Egypt exhibition, a series of mythological murders

ARCHAEOLOGIST DETECTIVE SERIES

THE EGYPTOLOGIST DETECTIVE SERIES.

Meet Daniel Cane, archaeologist and sometimes cruise Egyptologist, who finds himself digging for murder clues in Egypt instead of for buried artefacts.

MURDER ON THE NILE MYSTERY CRUISE

MURDER IN NUBIA

ARCHAEOLOGY OF MURDER

THE SHABTI DOLL MURDERS

THE SARCOPHAGUS

Adventure, mystery, fantasy. An archaeologist with a bow shoots an arrow into adventure...

In the modern age, Ryder an archaeologist in Egypt discovers a mysterious empty sarcophagus in a tomb. Then his Egyptologist partner Janet goes missing. He vows to go after her, even if it means journeying across the boundaries of reason and existence. Ahead of Ryder and his Ridgeback dog lies a pre-dynastic realm of myth: the mysterious Mistress of the Bow and Ruler of Arrows, the evil Lord Set, legions of animal-headed creatures, the venerable bird-man, the child Horus. And key to it all is the quest for the magical amulets of power. A life-and-death struggle is on at the edge of time. And the universe watches - and waits.

DYNASTY Zero

A primordial clash of humans, gods and demon demigods.

A young demigod boy Nemes, a future unifier of pharaonic Egypt, also known to history as Narmer, lived on the fault line between deity and humanity. It was a time of the gods and demigods, when the throne of the god Horus shook and the weak hands of men stretched out to catch the crown and seize the scepter of Egypt. The demon demigods did not stand by, but seized the moment to strike.

I, THE MUMMY

Preserved in the 'Tresses of Nephthys' - the sacred wrappings of linen woven by the goddess Nephthys and tied with the 'magic of knotted cords' of Isis, an immortal soldier hero rises to fight Egypt's greatest enemy - the ruthless Hyksos invaders and occupiers...

Action adventure thriller.

Awakened after a thousand years in a tomb sanctuary filled with weapons...

The Ancient Defender arises to fight against a ruthless oppressor.

The Hyksos have seized Egypt at a time of weakness following the Middle Kingdom, overpowering all with their superior technology of chariots, hardened bronze weapons and compound bows.

And they are now plundering Egypt for its forbidden secrets of power.

Can ancient history's most unlikely hero stop them and resurrect a divided land before the Hyksos can gain Egypt's most powerful and dangerous secret of all?

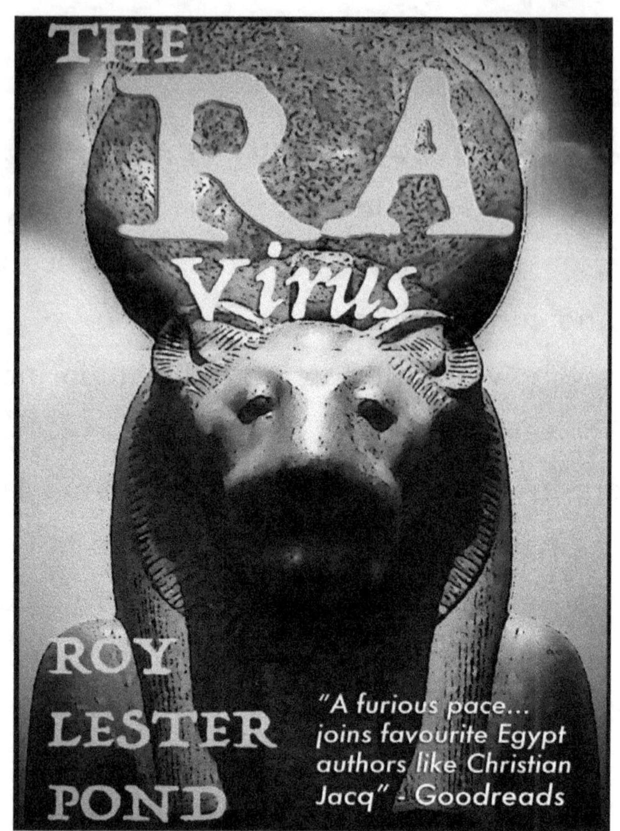

THE RA VIRUS

Is a vanished archaeology team member trapped in Egypt's ancient past during an age of terror – and sending warning messages to today?

'WARNING! ANCIENT GLOBAL THREAT...' the graffiti message appears in a newly found Egyptian tomb, along with a modern biohazard symbol.

What mysterious plague has hit the population of Egypt in the reign of Pharaoh Amenhotep III and his young co-regent, the sun-struck Akhenaten? Why is it seen as a judgement by the angry sun god Ra? An eleventh plague of Egypt?

Lucas, a physician and World Health Organisation expert on pandemics, must find its source and the antidote in time to save the ancient past and the future. Especially when his lover, Egyptologist Giulietta in the modern age, is exposed to the deadly contagion. Can he warn her in time and save her - and can they ever hope to be reunited?

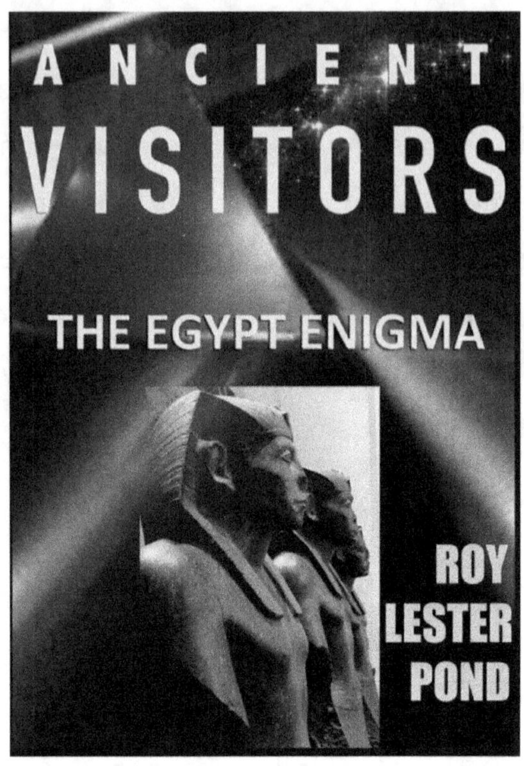

'Ancient VISITORS The Egypt Enigma'

In the field of ancient civilizations, 'visitors' meant one
thing to Egyptologist Rebecca Landers.
The controversial theory about the enigma of Egypt and
its advanced technological achievements.
Then came the surprising evidence... and a threat to the
world.
Suddenly she and her team were called on to span two
worlds on a dangerous archaeological quest like no

other.

Only they had the power to save history and the future.

EGYPT EXTRACTION

TIME JUMP ERA: 3 A.D.

MISSION: Save the Jesus child, a refugee in Egypt,

journeying with escaped family.

THREAT: modern day Islamic Time-Terrorists and

ancient assassins of Judean King Herod...

Time-travel terrorists... drones... attackers with assault weapons racing through the Nile's papyrus reeds... their target a boy king.

At stake, the future of civilization.

Standing in their way, two young time jumpers, Salome and Callen of the Anti Time-Terrorist Strike Force. They must stop a catastrophe that could affect billions of lives and the belief systems of the world. Sci-fi, ancient history and time-travel novella with a startling twist and revelation.

Plus AVATAR EGYPT

An ancient Egyptian simulator game turns deadly real.

EGYPT TRAP

Keep an eye on a mysteriously obsessed young wife visiting the archaeology sites of Egypt? How hard could that be?

A damaged ex-detective is hired to shadow a girl with painted eyes on a trip to Egypt...

Is she leading him step by step into a murder

conspiracy and the mystery of a lost ancient Egyptian queen?

Dan Loader reluctantly accepts the job. A damaged, former-detective from a police Art and Antiques unit, he is already traumatised by an ordeal at the hands of antiquity traffickers. Yet he desperately needs something to help him hold his life together and following the girl looks like a soft surveillance task, more so as he becomes increasingly drawn to her.

Rich, independent Kate Barnsdale is a beautiful, haunting young woman surrounded by an unmistakeable aura of ancient Egypt. Her obsession with a lost, mythic Queen from Egypt's 6th Dynasty seems to be taking over her life.

When she insists on travelling to Egypt alone to follow her mysterious urgings, her husband hires Dan to shadow her secretly and watch over her.

But is Dan being drawn step by step into a murder conspiracy that involves the secret of a mythic queen from Egypt's ancient past?

Crime and suspense with the mystery twist of ancient Egypt.

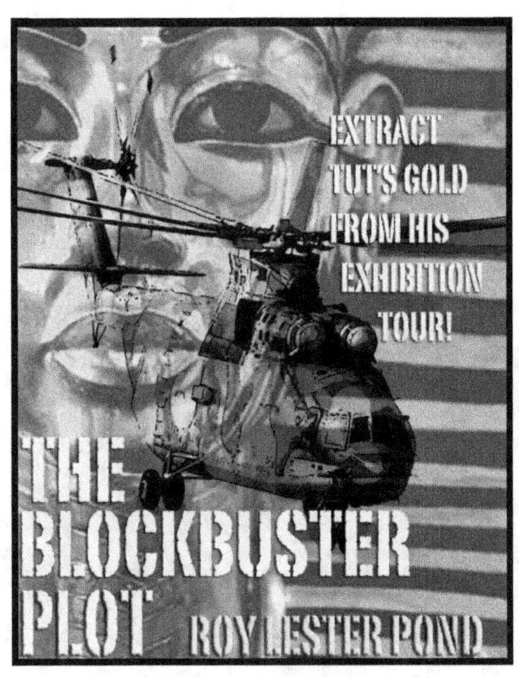

THE BLOCKBUSTER PLOT

The Boy King's Gold... a Blockbuster USA Tour... a dazzling display of criminal daring.

It was an outrageous plot:- Extract Tutankhamun's priceless gold on its blockbuster tour of the USA. *But who is the enigmatic mastermind behind the disappearing act and why have they done it?*

Will they demand a pharaoh's ransom for its return?

And what will become of a pair of US hostages, a museum Egyptologist and a female National Geographic feature writer traveling with the treasures?

A golden target, the most famous treasures in the world... *gone...* the fabulous golden artefacts of

Tutankhamun, about to appear in the USA in the biggest blockbuster exhibition since the world wide pandemic, have been stolen.

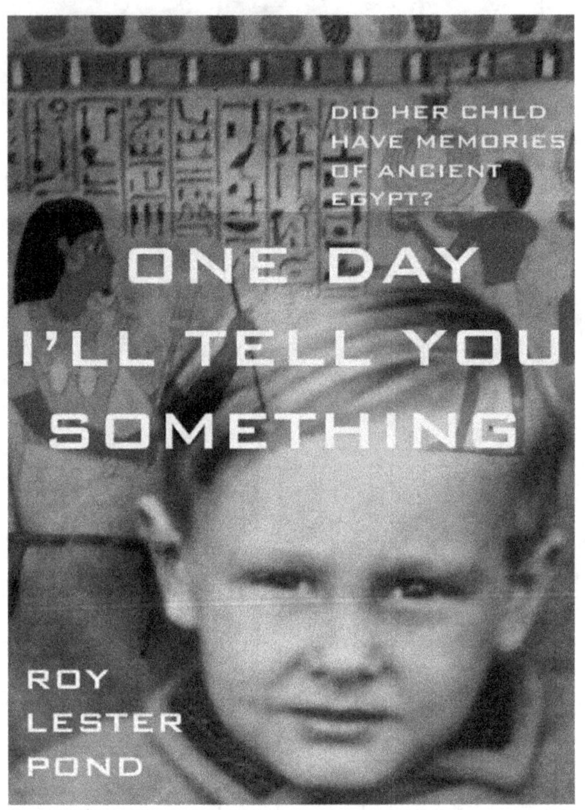

ONE DAY I'LL TELL YOU SOMETHING

A child obsessed with the ancient past, a young mother who discovers adventure..."

I remember Egypt," Cooper said gravely. "Long, long ago."

Her little boy was gorgeous, she thought, but his imagined past life could be a bit hard to take. Especially at 8.30 in the morning, when she was busy having a this-life crisis, running late for work and her eight-year old was about to miss his school bus.Then young single-mother Catherine meets a past life researcher and also a mysterious Egyptologist Simon Priestly and she and Cooper are off to Egypt on an extraordinary quest to follow a young boy's dreams... or are they actual memories of the ancient past?

What will they find and what will Catherine find as she warms to the impressive British Egyptologist as they uncover a shattering secret from Egypt's past? Disturbing and intriguing adventure fiction with a twist of the unknown.

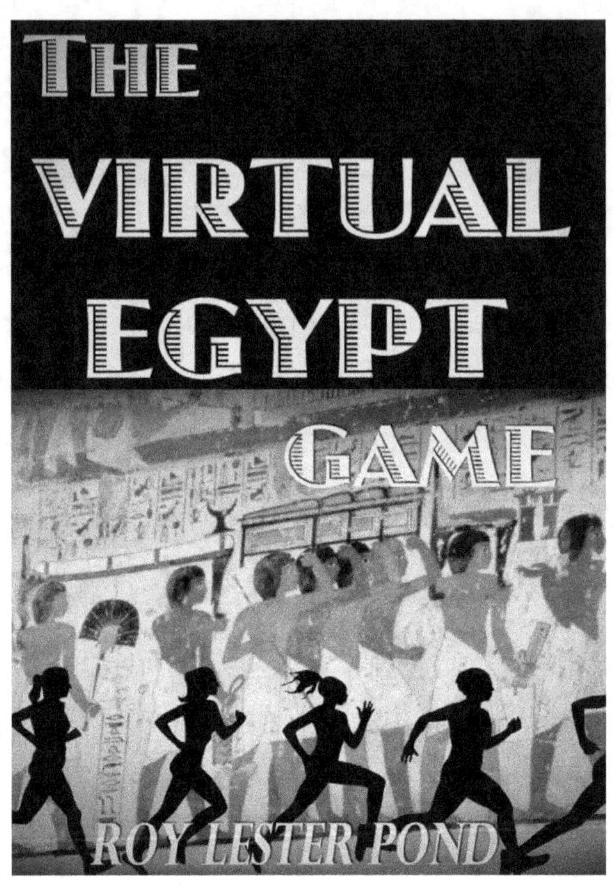

THE VIRTUAL EGYPT GAME - a group plays a deadly virtual reality running game inside a mysterious simulator of ancient Egypt's dangerous underworld. Then they start dying, for real.

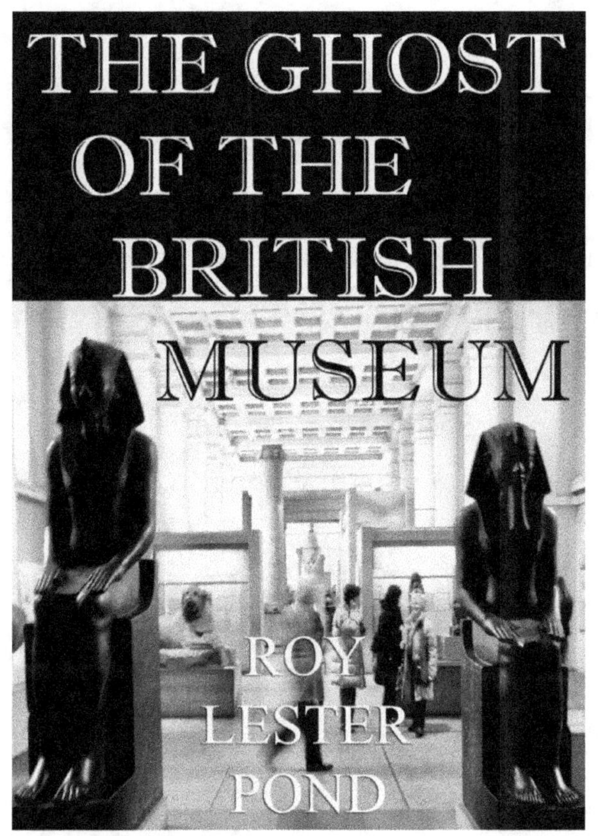

THE GHOST OF THE BRITISH MUSEUM

There is a certain statue in the Sculpture Gallery of the British Museum of the son of Rameses The Great, Egypt's most illustrious pharaoh.

The statue has an eerie attraction even today.

In the 1900s a London group known as The Society of Inner Light regularly conferred with the exhibit in the Egyptian Sculpture Gallery, convinced that it was a medium for metaphysical activity and emanated unseen forces.

She was an American historical writer visiting the British Museum's Egyptian Sculpture Gallery to research a new book.

He was a legendary and enigmatic prince from ancient Egypt who desperately needed to undo a terrible mistake.

Was the strange young man's sudden materialization before Madeline just 'cosplay', or the result of an attraction between two souls across time?

Would they share a mysterious quest on a journey through Egypt, and much more?

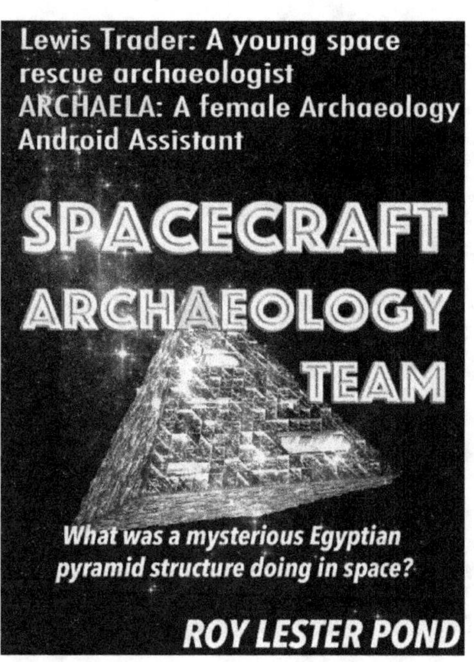

Lewis Trader: A young space rescue archaeologist
ARCHAELA: A female Archaeology Android Assistant
SPACECRAFT ARCHAEOLOGY TEAM
What was a mysterious Egyptian pyramid structure doing in space?
ROY LESTER POND

SPACECRAFT ARCHAEOLOGY Team

**Lewis Trader: A young space rescue archaeologist
ARCHAELA: A female Archaeology
Android Assistant**

**Was it a space mirage? A lost pyramid structure
abandoned in space...
In the future, a space archaeologist Lewis Trader
and his female archaeological android ARCHAELA
make a discovery.
A glowing ancient Egyptian-style pyramid floating
among the stars.
They begin a climb up guarded ramps inside the
structure amid rising levels of tension – their
progress challenged by mysterious, lethal
guardian sphinxes... leading to a startling
revelation.**

THE PRINCESS WHO LOST HER SCROLL OF THE
DEAD

2 Egypt Fantasy Titles in One.
1. The Princess Who Lost Her Scroll of the Dead
Her priceless Book of the Dead is swapped for a blank
one by a greedy royal scribe... How can Nefera find her
way through the dangerous gateways and guardians of
the Egyptian underworld without her magical spells -
her passport to the world beyond?
And who is the boy tomb robber Ipy, sharing her

journey? Is he alive, or dead?

2.

MUSEUM GHOSTS

Karoy and his companions - a squad of Egyptian wooden soldiers created to protect a tomb owner - arise when the Lady Tiy is stolen from the museum. Can they rescue her from the outside world?